JACOB'S LADDER

**Center Point
Large Print**

**This Large Print Book carries the
Seal of Approval of N.A.V.H.**

JACOB'S LADDER

JACKIE LYNN

CENTER POINT PUBLISHING
THORNDIKE, MAINE

This Center Point Large Print edition
is published in the year 2007 by arrangement with
St. Martin's Press.

Copyright © 2007 by Jackie Lynn.

All rights reserved.

The text of this Large Print edition is unabridged. In other
aspects, this book may vary from the original edition. Printed in
Thailand. Set in 16-point Times New Roman type.

ISBN-10: 1-60285-030-5
ISBN-13: 978-1-60285-030-9

Library of Congress Cataloging-in-Publication Data

Lynn, Jackie.
    Jacob's ladder / Jackie Lynn.--Center Point large print ed.
      p. cm.
    ISBN-13: 978-1-60285-030-9 (lib. bdg. : alk. paper)
      1. Camp sites, facilities, etc.--Fiction. 2. Nurses--Fiction. 3. North Carolina--Fiction.
    4. Large type books. I. Title.

PS3612.Y547J33 2007b
813'.6--dc22

2007010506

For Sandra Dixon,
who always makes me laugh out loud

ACKNOWLEDGMENTS

I gratefully acknowledge and appreciate all acts of encouragement shown to me. It is true what the wise folks say, "Kindness matters."

Thank you to Sally McMillan, Linda McFall, Nichole Argyres, and the editorial staff at St. Martin's Press.

We are climbing Jacob's Ladder
We are climbing Jacob's Ladder
We are climbing Jacob's Ladder
Soldiers of the cross.

JACOB'S LADDER

ONE

It was late when the old Ford pickup pulling a small travel trailer drove up to the office at Shady Grove Campground in West Memphis, Arkansas. Mary, the manager, always locked the door at 8:00 P.M., and any campers arriving after hours had to make their own arrangements regarding where to park. They were asked to put one night's payment in an envelope kept in a bucket by the front window, stuff the envelope through a slot in the door, and select a site from the large map pinned next to the after-hours directions.

Rose was usually the one to follow up by stopping at the site the next morning to find out how long the campers were planning to stay and whether or not they were satisfied with their hookups. Being late March, still well before the busy summer season, there were usually plenty of places from which to choose.

Jacob Sunspeaker was the driver of the old truck, a 1974 model, blue and white, with New Mexico tags. He came from the southern tip of McKinley County, west of El Morro and just beyond Ramah. He was of the Zuni tribe, lived in the pueblo, in a small house beside his sister and her family. He made jewelry—bracelets and rings mostly, some belt buckles, all silver with an inlay design—which he sold in Gallup.

13

That was where he bought his truck and trailer in the early nineties, when he was particularly productive and when the silver business was booming.

The trailer he was pulling, a Coachmen, was rusted on the bottom and its gray paint was peeling on the front and sides. It was a twenty-four-footer, with a double bed, a table, and extra storage—plenty of room for two people, more than was really needed for just one.

He took it to the market where he sold his bracelets and rings and over to Santa Fe and Albuquerque for the Indian Market and to some of the feast days at the pueblos, where he participated in the dances and got new ideas for his jewelry designs. He lived in it most of the summers, moving to his house only when the wind blew too hard, making it difficult to sleep or cook in a house on wheels.

The Coachmen suited Mr. Sunspeaker. Once he had received the vision that became his mission and when the knowledge of what he had to do became the sturdy place from which to hoist himself, he found the travel trailer was the best possible means of always being ready to relocate and visit the next nec-essary destination. He discovered that he liked the feel of being mobile, of having a dwelling that moved so effortlessly with him.

His sister teased him about taking up the habits of white people, so many of whom they saw driving their campers and trailers through the pueblo to get to the Hawikuh Ruins or Ojo Caliente, the hot springs near their homes. But her jokes never bothered him.

He told her that the ease of few belongings and the ability to move quickly were more the way of Indians, he having descended from a people who traveled as nature dictated.

The old Coachmen was dented in a few places, in need of a good wash, and two of the windows were cracked and covered with silver duct tape. Jacob Sunspeaker, however, was satisfied with both how it looked and how it pulled behind his old truck. He saw no need for an upgrade or a fresh coat of paint.

No one knew exactly what time he drove into the campground. Old Man Willie, who lived in one of Rhonda and Lucas's campers situated near the office, was usually the one who confirmed the times of arrival. Generally awake until very late, he stopped by the office every day and informed the manager on duty or one of the owners what time the after-hours visitors arrived.

That night, however, the raw, moonless night that Jacob Sunspeaker found his way from the interstate over to the river, Willie didn't hear the truck and the travel trailer pull in and stop. He was in bed, having eaten a very big dinner, and had been lulled to sleep by the extended winter chill and the black night of the March sky.

He was dreaming of violets and an old lover's smooth hands when the Coachmen pulled over to site number Thirty-four, one without hookups on the far right side of the campground, the grassy area near the

Mississippi and close to the uncleared part of the acreage.

Originally used for tents and people sleeping in their automobiles, that part of the campground had been closed for more than a year. The narrow piece of real estate owned by the Boyd couple jutted out farther into the Mississippi at that location and had been added to their purchase without their request. Over the years, the property had developed so many flooding problems that instead of trying to remedy them, Rhonda and Lucas had simply discontinued using that landing for camping sites.

Only hikers and the guests who enjoyed private fishing visited the spot, but there was still a driveway leading to it. Apparently, Mr. Sunspeaker had not paid attention to the map at the office and had driven down on the main road, past the curve that led into the park, and turned right onto the old driveway and into the closed-off area.

Willie had awakened because of a barking dog and was sad to be yanked away from a woman's arms and the dream he loved so much. Because he was awake, he did hear the other vehicle that pulled in just after Mr. Sunspeaker.

He peeked out the window just in time to see the one with the idling motor, the black SUV with unidentified license plates. He paid no attention to it, assuming it was an automobile belonging to a registered guest or that it was just someone visiting a friend. He knew cars came and went at Shady Grove as the campers enjoyed nightly excursions to Memphis and other places along the river.

Since he was not familiar with Mr. Sunspeaker and his journey to Arkansas, Willie had no way of knowing that the SUV was the same vehicle that had been parked on the pueblo for a week as the old man prepared for his journey, the same vehicle that had followed Jacob Sunspeaker out of New Mexico.

He also did not know the old man had seen the trouble coming to him in a dream in the form of a dark thundercloud and that Mr. Sunspeaker had pushed up his trip by more than a couple of days, trying to elude what he saw on the horizon.

Willie simply got back into bed, rolled over, and went back to sleep before noticing that the driver turned off his lights as the car headed down the main road behind the old truck and trailer and that there were at least three men inside, all dressed in black, two of them carrying guns. He pulled the covers tightly around his shoulders, wondering if the dream would come to him once more, hoping his lover had not drifted too far from his memories.

No one, not even Willie, knew that trouble, like a late winter storm, had passed through the gates of Shady Grove on the chilly night in March when the sky was pitch-black, the stars and the moon hidden behind clouds.

No one other than Willie heard the SUV as it entered the campground, and no one heard it leave within one hour's time. No one witnessed the old man struggle and finally fall. No one recognized the words that passed between his lips or the anguished way he prayed.

No one saw a thing.

TWO

The following day, Mary did not know there was a new camper on the grounds until she found the envelope on the floor in the office with fifteen one-dollar bills stuffed inside. She knew she hadn't seen anybody different on any of the sites when she drove around the grounds early in the morning, picking up trash in her golf cart. She had also already spoken to Willie, who made no mention of any latecomers as he handed his friend his bag of trash. He spoke only of the frosty night and the way the shadows had danced along the edge of the woods.

She took out the contents of the envelope, counted the money, considered where it might have come from, and logged in a receipt. She checked and sorted through the files and waited until Rose arrived to send her out to discover where the night's late arrival had camped. She started brewing the coffee, opened the reservation book, and sat down at her desk for her day's work. It wasn't long before she saw her friend walking up the drive and coming into the office.

"Somebody new here." Mary gave the report before any greeting. Since English was not her first language, she spoke in the clipped way to which Rose had grown accustomed.

"That's nice. Good morning to you, too," Rose replied as she walked in and shut the door. "It's cold. I thought the weatherman said we were going to have a warm front this week." She slid her hands up and down the sides of her arms. She was wearing only a lightweight jacket.

"Weathermen don't know about weather. I felt the cold in my shoulder yesterday. You should have asked me about what comes out front." She was flipping through the pages of reservations to see if she had missed one for the previous night.

"Ms. Lou Ellen has a doctor's appointment this afternoon. Since Rhonda and Lucas are gone, I said I would take her. I hope that's all right. You're going to be here, aren't you?" Rose unzipped her jacket and pulled it off. She hung it on the coat tree by the door.

"Where I go?" Mary blew out a breath of air.

"I don't know. You could have a date or something." Rose moved over to stand in front of the counter where Mary was working.

Mary rolled her eyes. "I don't see no reservation for anybody." She was not responding to Rose's suggestion.

The other woman walked behind the counter. "Why are you searching for one?"

"Because somebody stuck this in the door last night." She showed Rose the fifteen one-dollar bills. "I didn't see nobody new when I came in, and there's no reservation." She closed the book. "Willie didn't mention anybody coming in."

"Maybe they parked over in the last row. It's hard to see behind the trees." Rose stepped around Mary and checked to see if the coffee had finished brewing.

"You had your first cup yet?" she asked Mary as she walked toward the coffeemaker.

"Nah, I got busy and forgot."

"Well, let me sit down beside you and we'll drink together."

Rose wheeled the chair out from behind the counter and pushed it next to where Mary was standing. Then she reached for two mugs sitting under the window, wiped them out with a dish towel, and then poured coffee into each one.

"It's strange that Willie didn't hear anybody," Rose said as she handed Mary her mug and sat down beside her. "He doesn't miss much around here."

They both glanced out the front window, trying to imagine where the new camper was parked. They held the cups of coffee in their hands, waiting for them to cool.

"Maybe he already came and left," Rose said.

Mary considered the possibility. She took her first swallow, made a clucking noise with her tongue.

"That has happened, right?" Rose asked.

Mary opened the top drawer of her desk and found a sugar packet. She opened it and poured the contents in her drink. "Some," she said.

"Well, that's probably what it is if they aren't over in the last row." Rose nodded.

Mary stirred her coffee. There was a pause. "Ms. Lou Ellen get off her cane today?" she asked, tired of thinking about the mystery camper and his or her whereabouts.

"Yep. She's getting her walking license," Rose replied. "She's been immobilized and motorized and accessorized for longer than I thought she could manage. I suspect if that doctor doesn't release her today, she might just find a new use for that stainless-steel cane he gave her."

Mary smiled. Both women knew that Ms. Lou Ellen's hip fracture and surgery late in the summer the previous year had been a true hardship. The recovery period had taken longer than anyone expected, as there had been a few complications and the older woman was not one to sit around feeling content about being infirm and obeying orders. She had managed a difficult number of months.

"She say she good as new," Mary added." I tell her she good as old."

Rose laughed. She took a sip of coffee and placed the mug on the desk in front of her, then looked out the window again.

As if on cue, Ms. Lou Ellen had come out of her cabin and began walking on the path to the office. Both women watched her.

There was nothing odd about her being out and about, for she often came by to join her two friends for morning conversation. But Rose noticed right away that something was different about this trip Ms. Lou Ellen was making to the office. This time, she was not alone. Following behind her was a skinny, three-legged black dog. They hobbled together toward the office. The women were stunned to see such a sight because they both knew that Ms. Lou Ellen didn't have a dog and she had always made it perfectly clear that she did not like them very much.

"Well, my, my," Rose said to Mary as they stared at the older woman walking in their direction. She moved toward the office unhurriedly and carefully, using the cane as the doctor had ordered, while the dog, which the women in the office could now see clearly, limped behind her. The older woman appeared to be speaking to her new companion. She hesitated, as if she had thought of something, made a remark in the dog's direction, and laughed. Then she started walking again.

Ms. Lou Ellen made it to the front porch steps, slid the cane beneath her right arm, reached for the railing, and pulled herself up the four steps. She turned around to her new friend and he stumbled up next to her.

"Somebody open up and let us in. It's freezing out here." She had made it to the front door.

Rose stepped around the counter and opened the door. Ms. Lou Ellen moved in beside her, while the dog stood on the porch.

"It's all right, darling," she said to the animal. "These women are harmless."

The dog backed away and walked over to the corner of the porch. As if he had been commanded, he sat down and then slid his front paws forward, stretching into a prostrate position.

"Well, I guess somebody trained him right," Rose said as they both stared at the old mutt, who lay in the corner watching the women.

"I suppose," Ms. Lou Ellen replied as she turned around and headed into the office.

Rose pulled the door closed. She stood behind it, staring out the window at the dog.

"Where did he come from?" she asked as Rhonda's mother moved to the table in the center of the room and stood beside it. She was wearing a dark skirt, a thick wool sweater, and a raincoat. The hood fell across her eyes and she pulled it away.

"Who knows," she replied. "He just showed up at my door this morning, crying." She balanced the cane against the wall beside her and slipped her coat off. She threw it on the back of the chair and sat down.

"He sounded like an old hant. I heard him out there whining and carrying on, tried to shoo him off. Darn thing wouldn't leave." She nodded and winked in Mary's direction, her way of asking for coffee.

"He must have been out there an hour before I opened the door and finally peeked out." She settled in her chair as the other women listened. "When I did, well, of course, I realized right away who he is." She blew out a puff of air.

Rose and Mary waited.

"Well, friends, it's easy to see. Look in his eyes." She touched the sides of her hair. She was spent from her walk.

Rose peered through the screen. As if he had been called, the old dog lifted his head in her direction.

"Well, what am I saying? You certainly wouldn't recognize him," Ms. Lou Ellen said.

Rose turned to her friend, hoping that she was going to explain.

"You haven't known us long enough to recognize that memorable face."

Rose was curious.

"It's my ex-husband. Number two," she said very matter-of-factly.

Rose stared at her, waiting for more.

"If you had seen the man, you'd know," she said, waving her hands in the air. "Girls, it is Mr. Lester Earl Perkins returned from the dead to bring me trouble."

Mary poured Ms. Lou Ellen a cup of coffee, sprinkled some powdered cream in it, stirred it, and took it to her friend at the table.

"Just like that old devil to come back as a three-legged dog and hound me." She took the coffee with a smile. "Thank you, Mary dear."

"Phhtttt," Mary responded. "Your dead husband wouldn't be so quick to lay in a corner if he like you say he was." She glanced out the door at the dog. He was still lying quietly on the porch.

"Well, you're right about that," the older woman replied. "He'd be in this room licking the likes of both of you girls." She smiled.

"Really," Rose said, trying to take the conversation to a more serious level. "I've never seen this dog. Did he have a collar on?" She turned to Ms. Lou Ellen.

The older woman shrugged her shoulders. "I just gave him the bacon from my breakfast, dear. I did not handle him."

Rose opened the door and stepped out on the porch, moving over to the dog. She held out her hand and the animal sniffed it and then licked her palm. She held the dog's head up and noticed a thin, narrow red band around his neck. She pulled the collar around, but there were no tags. She patted his head and rubbed him under his neck and across his shoulders. She noticed the stump that used to be a fourth leg. There were no apparent recent wounds or markings. It seemed to her to have been an old injury.

"Looks like a mix of a Lab and maybe something else," she said to her friends as she stood up and walked back into the office. "Funny that we've never seen him before." She shut the door, reached over the counter, and got her coffee. "Wonder what happened to his hind leg."

"Well, if it is Mr. Lester Earl Perkins, he probably gnawed it off just to get my attention."

Mary rolled her eyes as she walked over to her desk behind the counter and sat down.

"Ms. Lou Ellen, I highly doubt that mutt is your dead husband." Rose sat at the table next to her friend.

"Say what you will." Ms. Lou Ellen smoothed her hair behind her ears, sounding particularly smug. "I just read in the *Enquirer* that Elvis roams over there across the river as an old white raccoon. And we all know the *Enquirer* reports truthfully." She lifted her brow and raised her chin, awaiting a reply.

There was none.

"So I cannot think it's impossible for Lester Earl to make his way from the other side, as well." She took another sip of her coffee. "They probably came together." She narrowed her eyes suspiciously.

Rose shook her head. "Well, whether he's your dead husband come back to haunt you or whether he's just an old stray, you have to decide what we're going to do about him."

"He stays," she said, sounding as if she had already thought through the decision. "I'm not about to put Lester Earl in the West Memphis Animal Shelter. He'd have every female dog howling like a coyote if I stuck him there." She turned her face toward the door and shouted, "Isn't that right, Mr. Perkins?"

The old dog jumped up from the corner and came to the door as if he had been called.

"You shouldn't play about spirits," Mary said,

watching the dog through the window. "Bad luck for campground."

"Oh for heaven's sake, Mary, we got so many ghosts hanging around this riverbank, one three-legged dog isn't going to bring us extra harm." Ms. Lou Ellen drank a few sips of her coffee.

"Besides, Mr. Perkins is not the harming kind. He's more of a lover than a fighter." She winked at the other women.

"Well, whatever he is, he's going to need watching after. You really want a dog?" Rose asked.

Ms. Lou Ellen shrugged her shoulders. "He'll just lie around here until he's bored. I expect he'll go wandering before too long." She drank some more from her mug.

"He looks kind of poorly to me," Rose said. "You want me to buy some food for him while we're out today?"

"Lovely idea, Rose. If I remember correctly, Mr. Perkins was particular to the shoulder roast, lean but tender. Maybe you could pick up a few pieces from the butcher shop in town."

"I was thinking more along the lines of a bag of dog chow." Rose replied as she leaned back in her chair.

"Dog chow?" Ms. Lou Ellen raised her voice. "Mr. Perkins, do you hear that? Dog chow?" she asked again, and the old mutt let out a whine. He was now sitting at the door watching.

Ms. Lou Ellen smiled and lifted her cup to her lips.

Rose shook her head. "Shoulder roast, lean but still tender."

Ms. Lou Ellen nodded. Then she stood up and slid her chair behind her. "Now, Rose dear, what time is my appointment with that good-looking bone doctor?"

Rose looked at her watch. "Nine-thirty," she replied. "You've got an hour to powder your nose and change into your fancy underwear." She finished her coffee and set down the mug, then took in a deep breath and continued. "I think I'll look around the park before we go, just to see if our late-night guest is still here." She faced her friend. "Do you need assistance back to your cabin?" she asked as she stood up from the table.

Ms. Lou Ellen waved her off. "I have my own companion, thank you, dear." She reached over and grabbed her cane, placing it in front of her. Then she pulled her coat around her and moved toward the door. "And just for your information, all my underwear is fancy."

Rose walked over and opened the door for Ms. Lou Ellen. "Of course it is. I'll pick you up a little after nine," she added.

"That's fine, dear. Tootle-doo." And she headed toward the porch and down the steps.

The old mutt moved aside, waiting for the woman. After Ms. Lou Ellen passed him, he wagged his tail and followed closely behind her.

Mary watched the two limp across the main campground entrance and over to the cabin where Ms. Lou Ellen lived. "That dog bring bad news," Mary said, drinking the last of her coffee and shaking her head.

"What makes you say that?" Rose asked. She had walked around the counter and was standing beside her friend.

"Just so," Mary replied. "I know missionary when I see him."

Rose looked puzzled. She thought for a moment. "I think you mean emissary."

"Whatever," Mary replied. "He come for reason."

"So you think that old dog is Ms. Lou Ellen's dead husband, too?" Rose asked, surprised at the other woman.

Mary shook her head, looking very serious. "He not come from the other side, but he travel here for something. He bring bad news."

"Okay, Mary," Rose said as she turned around and moved over to the coat tree and grabbed her coat. "A three-legged dog has brought us bad news." She slid it on as she headed outside. "By the way, how many dead ex-husbands does Ms. Lou Ellen have?"

Mary paused. She was thinking. "Five," she said. "Counting that last one she never divorced."

"For heaven's sake, we'll have to build a kennel if they all decide to come back." Rose shook her head and opened the door.

"And meat locker," Mary added.

Rose laughed. "Right, filled with lean, tender roast."

Ms. Lou Ellen and the dog had made it to the cabin. The office fell silent.

"Well, let me go and see about this mysterious one-dollar-bill camper," Rose said as she turned back to face her friend. "Maybe he'll give us more money and we can pay Lester Earl to take his troubles somewhere else." She smiled and the door closed behind her.

Rose made her way to the golf cart parked beside the office. She sat down and waved at Mary, who was watching out the window. She turned the key, popped the brake, and headed away from the office.

She drove first along the back side of the property, the row of sites nestled in the grove of river oaks. Old Man Willie was out front, and Rose greeted him with a wave of her hand.

The other two trailers that Lucas and Rhonda leased were in good shape, with no new rigs parked near them. She went past the pond where Thomas enjoyed fishing and glanced up the lane that meandered by the old quarry and out to his trailer. She smiled as she thought of her new lover.

She thought about driving over to see him but then remembered that he'd left early that morning to ride with his cousin into Fort Smith to buy a tractor. He wouldn't be home until the next day.

She drove all the way down to the river and then turned right, moving slowly past the campers parked in the best spots. She noticed her Casita, still on site number seventy-one, the same place she had been since she first made her way to Shady Grove Park almost six months earlier. The two sites beside her rig were empty, and then there was the large motor home with the couple from California, J.D. and Myrtle Hinshaw's travel trailer next to that one, and then the three rigs from the group from Manitowoc, Wisconsin, on their way south to Brownsville, Texas. One of the couples was just returning from a walk around the property, and Rose greeted them as she drove past them.

It was cold and she wanted to return to the office, but she huddled down inside the cart, trying to get out of the wind. She went up and down the three roads that accessed all the sites near the Mississippi River but did not see any new camper, only the same vehicles that had been parked there the previous day.

She turned down the river road again and was returning to the office when she noticed Ms. Lou Ellen's dog standing in the center of the driveway that led to the part of the property that was closed to campers.

Rose pulled the golf cart toward the dog, and as she got near him, he jumped up and turned, running down the drive. Without knowing what to expect, she decided to follow the old mutt. She stepped on the gas pedal and drove down the dirt drive. She didn't see the truck and the Coachmen until she was right in front of them. She hit the brake and sat in the cart, staring at the rig, while the old dog stood at the sliding trailer steps and barked.

Apparently, Rose thought, surprised to find the travel trailer in that section of the campground, Mr. Lester Earl Perkins had arrived at Shady Grove in a Coachmen. And he was not traveling alone.

THREE

Rose stepped out of the golf cart as the dog wagged his tail and barked.

"What is it, old guy?" she said as she walked toward the camper. "This your home?"

She headed toward the front steps, stopping to rub the dog on the head. "Whose idea was it to park over here?" she asked as she stood up, glanced around, and finally knocked on the door.

"Hello," she called out. "Anybody home?" There was no response except the whining of the dog.

The camper had been backed into the small space. There were no tracks coming in from behind, just the ones in front of the rig, a wide curve to the right, and then a straight movement to the rear, stopping in the position in which it now rested.

As she stood waiting at the steps, Rose did notice, however, another set of tracks following up the drive.

At first, she thought that maybe the driver had pulled up and backed in a couple of times before getting his rig like he wanted it; that perhaps he or she had even realized that this was not part of the working campground and was going to exit. When she looked more closely, however, she realized that the other tracks were different. The tires were wider, a tighter tread. There were two vehicles that had driven into this area the previous night.

Rose turned to examine the area behind her and could make out the departing tracks that returned to the drive and led out the main entry. She faced the door, puzzled at where the other vehicle was and how it had also entered and departed without anyone hearing it. She checked her watch, wondering if she was waking the traveler, shrugged her shoulders, and knocked again.

"Hello, is anybody home?" she called out as politely as she could.

She tried to peek through the window on the door, but she couldn't see anything but a pale blue curtain that covered the glass completely. She waited and then knocked again. There was not a single noise coming from inside.

She moved down the steps and walked around the rig. She could see that there had been no attempt to unhook the truck from the rig, that the driver had only backed in and then placed two large stones behind the rear tires, a temporary means to secure the camper.

Even though the trailer and the truck appeared to be old, there was a good strong ball and hinge attachment on both vehicles that appeared relatively new. The silver finish was not rusted like the axle on the trailer and there were no chips or scratches to show age or wear. There was also an additional pin and fastener, found only on the newer models, so that Rose could see that the owner had updated the hauling features, apparently planning for a long trip.

The safety chain was thick, at least four-inch links, and it wrapped around the hitch on the truck and under the extension that was bolted to the camper. It, too, looked new. It seemed that the latest Shady Grove tenant had taken extra care to travel safely from New Mexico all the way to West Memphis, Arkansas.

Rose read the license plate on the truck. There was nothing significant about it. The bright yellow plate with the parallel red lines pointing in all four directions was dusty and bent. She saw that the sticker had expired at least four months earlier, but it was hard to read, since the paper had been torn and replaced.

She knelt down and noticed a leak under the engine block, a small puddle near the front of the vehicle. The liquid was dark, black like oil, she thought. She wondered if it was the engine trouble that had led the campground guest to park where he did, thinking that he was making the attempt to be courteous and not stain the large concrete pads on the other sites. She certainly did not know any other reason for the camper to be in that location.

As she stood up, she peered again around the empty lot. She considered that maybe the trailer owner had taken a walk or was down at the riverbank fishing, that maybe he had gone searching for the dog. She saw no one moving about on this side of the camp-ground.

She turned again to the trailer, and that was when she saw a small opening in the curtain in the rear window of the camper. She was hesitant at first, but then she moved over to it and gently knocked on it. She guessed that this would have been the window right above the bed, and again she hoped she was not waking anyone up.

She pressed her face against the glass, cupping her hand around her eyes as she peeked in.

It was dark inside and it took a minute before her eyes adjusted. When they did, what she saw immediately concerned her. Either the visitor at Shady Grove was the most cluttered person she had ever encountered or the trailer had been ransacked. Although she couldn't see the entire interior space of the old Coachmen, what she could make out were household items—pots and pans, linens and clothes—all tossed around.

The small kitchen table was overturned, as was the back bed. Sheets and pillows were thrown about. Cabinets were standing open and cookware and canned goods were strewn across the camper floor. It was a mess, and Rose, concerned that someone was inside and had been hurt, began rapping on the window.

"Hello! Is there anybody in there?" she yelled. Then she pressed her face against the glass again. This time, she tried to see as much of the inside of the trailer as she could. And when her eyes panned around the second time, she noticed something sticking out from beneath the narrow table.

It was an arm, thin and brown, the palm facing up. It extended from underneath the broken piece of furniture.

"Oh Lord," Rose screamed as she hurried away from the camper, falling against the rear of the truck. The dog had been standing at her feet, and in her gruesome discovery, she'd tripped over the three-legged mutt. She leaned against the truck to regain her balance.

She ran around to the front steps and tried opening the door. It was locked. She pushed against it, without much luck of forcing it open. So she jumped down, ran back to the truck, and picked up one of the rocks at the rear tire. She hurried again to the front door and, using the stone, broke the window. She dropped the rock and quickly reached inside, turning the lock. Then she pushed the door and moved inside.

It was worse than what she had thought. The place was destroyed inside. It was more than just clutter or things becoming unsettled from a bumpy ride. It was evident that this mess had been created, that someone had deliberately set about to cause damage.

Once inside, walking about and making her way through the mess, she immediately knew that she was compromising the scene, something her father, a police captain, had constantly drilled into her head

36

when he was preaching to her about good police work.

Rose, however, a nurse by profession, knew the most important thing at that moment was trying to find the person who belonged to the arm she had seen sticking out from underneath the table.

She made her way through the pile of boxes and personal belongings to the small dining table and yanked it up, throwing it toward the rear of the camper. There was a bedsheet beneath it. She pulled that away, and there lay a man, older, maybe seventy or seventy-five, dead, she thought, for more than a few hours.

Having worked in health care for all of her adult life, Rose quickly checked for a pulse, found none, and then tried to determine the nature of the camper's injuries. She felt both his left wrist and then the carotid artery in his neck. There was nothing. And she could tell by the slight stiffness in his limbs and the blue tinge across his lips that he had arrived late at Shady Grove Park the previous evening and had died soon after. There was no way he could be revived.

While she was trying to find a pulse at his neck, she noticed the marks circling just below his chin. Large welts, shaped like the tips of big fingers or thumbs, were raised and red; and there had been enough pressure placed on the old man's windpipe that she was sure it was crushed. She assumed that a murderer had used his own hands as the weapons.

Rose assessed the situation and surmised that the

old man who had arrived at Shady Grove had been strangled to death by somebody he'd brought with him, or by somebody who was already there, or by somebody who had followed him to his campsite. She was alarmed, sad, and bewildered, and without hope of changing what had happened there in the empty, narrow landing at Shady Grove, she sat down beside the man while the dog that had probably come with him stood at his feet.

She knew that there was nothing to do but return to the office and call the sheriff. She sat only a few minutes, considering the dead man's life and death, wondering where he'd been going and who was waiting for him there. She thought of his family and loved ones, of their grief and loss, and of the evil that had lurked so near to her own tiny residence.

She knelt again above the man and placed the sheet across his face, a gesture of respect, and noticed a broad band across his wrist, an area of skin that was not tan like the rest of his arm. It looked to Rose to be a spot that marked the bearings of a piece of jewelry, a watch maybe, that was now missing. Rose slid her fingers across the pale stretch of skin and then gently laid his arm to his side.

She stood up and searched around the camper. The old man didn't seem to have anything valuable with him. What she could make out of the personal belongings that had been ransacked, all appeared scanty, outdated, and inexpensive.

The dog began to whine, and Rose turned to the

black mutt. "I guess you know what happened," she said. "But you aren't likely to tell." She reached down, petting his head.

"So, we better go call the law." She squatted down again, facing the dead man.

"Looks like Mary was right," she said to no one. "We got some trouble here."

She got up and walked over to the door, held it open while the dog limped out. She pulled the door shut and stood staring at the camper and the truck, the place of such tragedy.

As she headed down the steps, moving in the direction of the golf cart, she noticed something in the grass about twenty feet from her mode of transportation. She hadn't seen it when she pulled in. It was a small thing, but it shone in the sun, like a mirror or a piece of tin. She walked over to it, knelt down, and realized it was a bracelet. She picked it up and turned it over in her hands.

It was silver, a cuff style, a broad band with intricate designs engraved in it. There were small pieces of blue-green turquoise lining both the top and the bottom edges, one large stone pressed and set in the middle. It was not that old, Rose could tell, but it was very well made. It was thick and heavy, nothing like the thin, slick bracelets that she saw most people wearing.

The designs were the same as the petroglyphs she had read about in an article about prehistoric times. They were designs that people found on stones and sides of mountains in the Southwest, symbols of animals and clans, maps and shields.

She held the piece of jewelry in her hand, rotating it, studying it, and as she tried to understand the meanings of the engravings, she realized that the bracelet was the same size as the faded place on the dead man's wrist.

More than likely, Rose thought, the killer stole the bracelet and then dropped it when he got outside the camper. He was likely in a hurry or had his hands full of other things and it just fell into the grass. He probably doesn't even know he lost it, she thought. And yet, she was almost sure that this was the only thing of value that the old man could have had.

Could the thief be so careless? she wondered. And if he killed a man for this piece of jewelry and then lost it, might he return to Shady Grove and try to find it?

The last question worried Rose. And quickly, as if she thought someone could be watching, she stuck the bracelet in the front pocket of her jacket, got into the cart, and hurried to the office.

This time, the old dog did not follow behind. He stood at the trailer and watched the woman leave, then turned and lay down at the foot of the sliding steps.

Rose drove quickly to the entrance of the campground and parked at the front steps of the office. She ran inside, where Mary had stood up from her desk and come around the counter after hearing Rose speeding up the drive.

"Call the sheriff," Rose said. Her tone was calm but imploring. "The one-dollar-bill customer was in the old tent section. One of the sites off the road, a back-in, one without any hookups. A truck and Coachmen from New Mexico."

She took a breath as Mary hurried around to her desk and picked up the phone to dial the number.

"He was an old man. Indian. The dog came with him." She felt flushed, even though she hadn't run a step.

She stopped as Mary asked for the sheriff; then the office manager slid the receiver away from her mouth and raised her shoulders at Rose as if raising a question. "What I say to Sheriff Montgomery?" she finally asked.

"Tell him there's been a murder," she replied. "The man's dead."

FOUR

Did you touch everything in the trailer?" Sheriff Montgomery asked as he stepped over pots and pans, following Rose as she walked in front of him over to the dead body.

He sighed as he looked around. Murders always made him cranky and tired. It hadn't been too terribly long since the Franklin murder, and he'd just started to feel relaxed, when now this, another unexplained death, occurred down by the Mississippi River.

"No, I just pushed aside the table, pulled away that sheet, and tried to see if there was anything I could do," she told him.

She knew that the sheriff was still displeased with her from the first time they'd met. "I touched the sheet, of course," she explained. "I thought maybe he wasn't dead, that I could help."

When Rose first arrived at Shady Grove and heard about the death of Lawrence Franklin, a local funeral home owner, she became convinced that the sheriff was involved in foul play, that he was somehow partly to blame. She was wrong and had apologized, and they had seen each other lots of times in the past months, at town events, restaurants. They had been cordial to each other, but Rose thought the lawman still seemed to hold a grudge against her.

She had mentioned it once to Thomas, told him that she thought Sheriff Montgomery didn't like her. He told her the sheriff acted like that with everyone, that his hard edge was what helped him maintain his authority and that there was nothing unique in how he treated Rose. She had listened to what Thomas had said and tried to believe him, but she'd never fully accepted that Sheriff Montgomery didn't have something against her.

"Tell me again how it is that you found the dead guy." He had made his way to the body and was kneeling beside the traveler. He studied the man's face. There was nothing odd about his features.

Rose was close behind him. "I was out trying to find the late-night arrival. Somebody had left the money and Mary couldn't find where he was camped. I was out searching for him."

The sheriff stood up and bumped into her. She quickly moved aside, trying to get out of his way.

He yelled past Rose to the deputy standing outside the trailer. "Roy, get the coroner over here and make sure this area is secure. Close it off all the way to the driveway. And use the police-line tape this time, not the property markers." The sheriff turned back to the body.

"He was strangled," Rose said after waiting for him to finish his instructions. "There are bruises all along his neck." She paused. "It seems like a terrible way to be killed," she added, mostly to herself.

"All ways are terrible when it comes to being killed," the sheriff replied, sounding particularly tired.

"I thought Lucas didn't have campers out here," he added as he stepped around Rose.

She leaned very far against the wall. "He doesn't. I don't know how the old man got over here." She turned and looked again at the dead man's face. "He's Indian, don't you think?" she asked.

"I don't know. Indian, Mexican. Who knows, coming from over there?"

Sheriff Montgomery had also taken note of the license plate. He knew the camper was registered in New Mexico.

He reached into his pocket, pulled out a notebook, and began writing some things down.

"I think he's definitely Indian," Rose said softly, noticing the straight gray hair tied in a ponytail, the wide forehead, and the thin lips.

He appeared different from the Native Americans she had met when she worked briefly in Lumberton, North Carolina, those from the Lumbee tribe. They were darker, with broader lips and noses. The dead man seemed to have more of an Asian influence, tight features and a lighter complexion.

"How will you contact his family?" she asked.

"From the plates. I'm having them run now," he replied. "Tell me again what time you broke into the place," he said gruffly, turning toward Rose.

"I don't know." She held out her arm to look at her watch. "Not more than half an hour ago." Then she remembered Ms. Lou Ellen's appointment. It was after 9:00 A.M.

"Oh my goodness. I'm supposed to take Ms. Lou Ellen to the doctor." She faced the sheriff. "Can I run down to the office and make sure she gets a ride?"

"Just go ahead and take her yourself. I'll get your statement when you return." He stuck the notebook in his pocket. "I got a lot of other things to do." Then he glanced around the camper again.

"You didn't take anything from the trailer or find anything suspicious, did you?" He narrowed his eyes at the woman.

Her hand was in her jacket pocket and she felt the

44

bracelet. She knew she should tell the sheriff about having found it. She knew it was just the kind of thing he was asking her about, but something kept her from speaking of it. She shook her head, figuring she wasn't lying, since the bracelet had not been inside the trailer. She bit her lip, knowing that she was stretching things in order to rationalize her behavior.

She had no idea what she planned to do with the piece of jewelry; she wasn't a thief by nature. It just seemed to her that it bore some secret regarding this man's arrival and his murder, and she wanted to find out for herself.

"Then just come by the office when you're back." He shook his head. "What is it with you and this place?" he asked, referring to the other murder in which she had become involved, when she first moved to Shady Grove, that of Lawrence Franklin.

Rose shrugged her shoulders, trying to maintain her stance of innocence. "Must just be lucky," she replied.

"More like unlucky," the sheriff responded.

"I guess," she said, but she was thinking it was more of a gift than a curse to be involved in these events.

In spite of being put in danger and injured when she stumbled upon the killers of Mr. Franklin a few months earlier, she knew she would never have found her place in West Memphis, never have found her home, if it hadn't been for the grave circumstances that occurred when she arrived.

45

Her relationship with Mr. Franklin's mother and the friendships she had made with Rhonda and Lucas, Mary, Ms. Lou Ellen, not to mention Thomas, had been worth every moment of fear and doubt she had suffered. And standing in the dead man's trailer, near the body of a dead Indian from New Mexico, the premonitions she was experiencing were both oddly familiar and comforting.

She knew she was about to encounter another exciting adventure. She pulled her hand out of her pocket and smiled at the sheriff.

"Well, I hope you figure things out," she said as she walked toward the door.

Then she stopped and turned around. "Do you think he meant to come here, or was he just passing through?" she asked, referring to the dead man.

"I suspect it was a little of both," he replied.

Rose thought the sheriff had something else to add. She waited as the lawman looked out the window. She followed his eyes to the banks of the Mississippi River, the water brown and choppy in the early-spring wind.

"She pulls a lot of folks here," he added, referring to the river. "Whether they mean to come and stay or whether they just want to see her, walk along the bank, float on top, she calls many a lost soul to her shores."

Rose smiled at that. She knew that she was one in the long line of those souls.

"There's a lot she tells to some folks," he remarked,

"and a whole lot she just keeps to herself well beneath those curved whitecaps."

Rose followed the sheriff's eyes and watched the water dance in the breeze. She peered again at the lawman and nodded, remembering her own yielding to the Mississippi, the way she camped at the edge, the measure of comfort she found in her wide brown arms.

"Yeah," she responded. "I suspect one way or another, we're all meant to be here." She turned around and faced the dead man. "I guess he had his reasons, too." Then she blew out a breath and walked a couple of steps toward the door.

"I'm sorry if I compromised your crime scene," she said to the sheriff. She thought he appeared weary, that maybe the job was getting to him, that in some way he was too sensitive for such work.

"It's not a problem, Rose," he said, sounding almost fatherly. "Go take Lou Ellen to the doctor and meet me at the station." He hesitated. "You didn't do anything wrong."

Rose studied the older man. His words of pardon were enough to ease her guilt. She opened the door to the camper and found the dog standing at her feet. She bent down and scratched under his chin. "I guess you'll be staying with us after all."

He wagged his tail and followed behind the woman as she made her way to the office.

FIVE

Did you show Sheriff Montgomery?" Ms. Lou Ellen was examining the bracelet that Rose had taken from the area outside the camper.

Rose drove ahead through the stoplight once it changed from red to green. She turned to see her friend holding the piece of jewelry that she had taken out of her pocket to give her. She shook her head.

Ms. Lou Ellen raised her eyebrows. She seemed surprised.

"I know," Rose said before the older woman could comment. "It was wrong of me. I'm going to hand it over to Sheriff Montgomery when I go to the station." She faced the road. "There was just something about it that made me want to keep it for a little while."

Ms. Lou Ellen hummed a reply as she flipped the bracelet over and traced the engraved symbols with her fingertip. "Maybe it's this luscious piece of turquoise." She held it close to her eyes to analyze it. "It is difficult to find gems this unspoiled anymore."

The older woman was right. It was a beautiful stone. The color of it was a rich watery shade of blue, unlike any piece of turquoise that Rose had ever seen. Thick and smooth from hours of polishing, it fit perfectly in the center of the bracelet and reminded the woman of a small reflection of the desert sky held in the pool of deep canyon water.

"And the engravings are simply divine." She traced the symbols. "I expect this is Hopi or Zuni, not Navajo. They tend to do more of a stamp than inlay."

She faced Rose, who seemed a bit puzzled. "I worked in a jewelry store before I married for money," she added as an explanation. "We had a very good selection of Native American jewelry." She held out the bracelet to Rose, who had stopped at another intersection.

"What do you think the symbols mean?" Rose asked as she pulled ahead cautiously. She did not take back the piece of jewelry.

"These are sequenced in such a way, they look like they tell a story." The older woman kept it in her hands. She noticed again the different symbols. "Some of these are very old," she said, remembering some of the more common symbols she'd seen on jewelry. She recalled bears and bear claws, classic signs of strength, corn and squash, the crops they grew, signs of clans and gods. But none of these was found on the dead man's bracelet. She held it up to her eyes once again.

"This, I believe, is an old sign of the sun," she said, pointing to two symbols placed on both sides of the turquoise. Rose peered down to see what she was describing.

"Usually, the sun is designed as a circle with a face placed in the lower quadrant just underneath a horizontal line stretching from side to side."

49

This carving, Rose saw, was a small circle within a larger circle.

"I've only seen it in books, never on a piece of jewelry," Ms. Lou Ellen remarked.

"Now the spiral shown here"—she pointed to a carving on the bracelet—"is the common sign for migration."

The younger woman looked again to see what her friend was explaining.

"And these"—she pointed to thick, crooked lines running parallel—"I would say these are map signs, trails or something like that."

She shook her head. "There were so many things to recognize. Most of the tourists just wanted a memorable story about the four-dollar earrings they were buying for somebody back home. Half the time, I just made things up." She laughed. "I can be very creative when I'm trying to sell something.

"Anyway, I don't recognize a lot of these. Like this one?" She held up the bracelet, pointing to two rows of dots, small lines connecting them in three places. "I would guess that this is rain, but usually the symbol includes two columns of three small parallel and horizontal lines. I don't know what the small marks in the middle would be. And this one . . ." She turned the bracelet over.

There was a box, completely dark and carved out. "And this circle with half of it darkened and the other half bearing small dots . . . And these two with the box and the dot and these unidentifiable figures. . . ."

She shook her head and put the bracelet in the console between them.

"You'll need to find somebody who specializes in old petroglyphs to understand some of this." She sighed. "I mean, if that's why you kept it?" She flipped down the visor and began to check her lipstick in the mirror.

Her comment sounded to Rose like a question and she suddenly felt defensive in needing to provide an answer.

"Well, I didn't keep it because I plan to sell it or wear it or anything like that."

Rose felt the need to justify her actions even though she knew Ms. Lou Ellen was not judging her. Ms. Lou Ellen was just not that kind of a woman.

"Of course you didn't, dear," she said sincerely. "You are just drawn to the great mysteries of life."

Rose remembered how she had taken the gold coin from Thomas's trailer, the way she was pulled into the other unexplained death at Shady Grove. She knew her friend was referring to her participation in that event.

"It can't be helped." The older woman studied herself in the mirror. She reached down and retrieved the lipstick from her pocketbook. "I was married to a man like that," she added.

"The dog?" Rose asked, glad for a chance to lighten up the conversation. She made the turn into town.

"Oh, for heaven's sake, of course not. I'm speaking of Henry Matthew Oliver. Now, was he number four or number five?" she asked herself, then waved away the question. "Doesn't matter. I just remember how he had to know the reason for everything, always searching for clues and answers. The man couldn't bear hearing the response 'I don't know.'"

Rose made her signal, headed left down Main Street, and proceeded in the direction of the doctor's office.

"What kind of work did he do? Was he a police detective or a private investigator?" she asked.

"No, dear. He was a pastor." She dabbed the bright red color on her lips. "Presbyterian." She smacked, sliding her lips across each other. She turned, to see that Rose had a surprised look on her face.

"I know, it's hard to believe that for a brief stretch in my life I was a preacher's wife," she said. "And yet, it's true. I even played the organ," she added with a bit of flair in the tone of her voice.

"Anyway, Henry wasn't very good at his work." She flipped the visor back in place as they pulled into the parking lot. "You know, faith demands loyalty without appropriate reason or explanation." She touched at the sides of her hair. "Henry grew to be tiresome to himself with all his doubts and queries, and even more so to his congregation. You know how church folk desire definitive and sound answers from their clergy." She peered toward the door of the office.

"Anyway, he was about to be run out when he eventually left the pulpit and became a wine supplier. That was about the time I quit drinking." She winked. "Eventually, we had nothing in common."

Rose pulled into a parking space.

"I used to love my wine," she explained. "Whites mostly. Crisp and fragrant. We spent hours together discussing the finer qualities of chardonnay, the bouquet of pinot noir. It used to excite me." She blew out a long breath.

There was a pause before she spoke again.

"Funny, don't you think?" the older woman asked. "Why it is that some people can't be comfortable with the things they can't explain?"

Rose considered her friend's observation as she turned off the ignition.

"The poor pastor drove himself insane trying to find answers to questions he hadn't even yet asked. Whatever is the judgment behind that kind of never-ending restlessness?"

Rose shrugged her shoulders. "Maybe some of us just like to think we can get a handle on things if we understand them, that if we can make sense of the small things, then the bigger things won't have the power to overwhelm us."

"See, that was the difference between me and Henry. I prefer being overwhelmed," Ms. Lou Ellen offered. "It is so much more interesting than the alternative."

"What's the alternative?" Rose asked as she pulled the keys out and placed them in her purse.

"Being underwhelmed," Ms. Lou Ellen replied. She

reached for the seat belt to unbuckle it. "I find the greatest fulfillment in life comes in the acceptance of how much I do not know and then just bathing in the delight of sitting still with the mystery of it all."

"Do you think I kept the bracelet because I need an answer to why the old man was killed? That I'm unable to be comfortable in not knowing?" Rose turned in her seat to face her friend.

"Certainly not," Ms. Lou Ellen said. She reached for the door handle. "I think you took it because you're a pillager and a thief." She smiled.

Rose appeared stunned.

"I'm teasing, dear." She reached over and patted the younger woman on the hand. "You must learn to appreciate my sophisticated brand of humor." Then she picked up the piece of jewelry and placed it in Rose's palm.

"You took the bracelet because you think it will reveal a clue as to why life sometimes ends so violently. You took it because somewhere deep down in your soul, you want desperately to understand how trouble can determine the journey of a man." She patted her hand. "Or a woman."

She closed the younger woman's fingers over the piece of jewelry. "Certainly this man's belonging bears an old and painful story, and I suspect it will explain what brought him to us." She pulled away. "But it will not give you all the answers you seek. Nothing ever does."

The older woman pulled open the door and waited

while Rose walked around the car and handed her the cane.

"Rose dear," Ms. Lou Ellen said as she shifted her legs around and stood up beside the car, "keep the bracelet until tonight. Copy down the pictures of the symbols so you can take them to the library tomorrow and reference them. When darkness falls, return the jewelry to where you found it and let one of the lawmen think he's brilliant, having discovered it all by himself."

"Yeah, but," Rose objected, but she was unable to finish before she was interrupted.

"The bracelet is not why the old man was killed," the older woman said confidently. "It's a nice piece of jewelry, good stones, good silver, but even I can see that it isn't worth a lot of money. And since we've both now compromised it with our fingerprints, it is no longer a clue to his murder."

Ms. Lou Ellen angled the cane between them. "It is, however, probably a clue to his life's journey, maybe a clue to everyone's life's journey. And Rose"—she moved closer to the younger woman—"somehow I think that's likely to be more significant to your questions."

She stepped around her friend and headed to the office door while Rose hurried to catch up.

SIX

Rose and Ms. Lou Ellen enjoyed milk shakes at the local burger joint before they returned to Shady Grove and before Rose made her way to the sheriff's office. It was a means of celebration that Ms. Lou Ellen was finally able to walk on her own, released from canes and walkers and even physical therapy. She had, however, made a request for another month's rehabilitation because she had grown quite fond of her therapist.

"That strapping young man just makes me feel better," she had said to the doctor, who recognized what he was doing was an abuse of his power but who agreed to write the order.

"One more month," he'd said as sternly as he was able, then handed her the prescription form. She had agreed with a wink.

After she let Ms. Lou Ellen out at her house, the three-legged dog patiently waiting for her at the door, Rose stopped by her trailer to pick up her cell phone and check messages before she headed back into town. Thomas had called, saying he missed her and that he would be in Fort Smith for an extra day. His cousin was having a difficult time picking out a tractor and wanted to check out a few more dealerships.

Rose was anxious for Thomas to return so that she

could discuss the murder with him, hear his thoughts about the bracelet and his ideas about why someone would have killed the old man.

She changed from the long-sleeved shirt she had been wearing and put on a short-sleeved one, keeping the light jacket. It was not as cold as it had been in the early morning, since the sun had come out and the day was getting on.

She took the bracelet out of the jacket, examined it, and then returned it to the front pocket. Then she drove back into town, thinking again about Ms. Lou Ellen and laughing at her friend for talking the doctor into letting her have another month of physical therapy and the way the older woman had pranced into the waiting room after the examination. She'd paraded to the far wall, turned, held both arms out to her sides, and walked like a fashion model on a runway, finally stopping in front of Rose's chair. The younger woman smiled, remembering the delightful scene, and was glad to see Ms. Lou Ellen fully recovered. She had been her primary caregiver for the entire time of the healing process and it pleased the nurse to see that her duties would no longer be needed.

When she arrived at the downtown office, Sheriff Montgomery was not back from lunch. She was actually relieved that she would not have to see him, since she got to his office much later than she had planned. She walked into the building and was greeted by a receptionist, who was sitting at a large desk just by the door.

The older woman called a deputy to the front and Rose was then instructed by the young man—Roy, she thought his name was—to go to the conference room and write a statement of what she had witnessed. He told her to jot down everything she had seen and done regarding the discovery of the dead man, beginning with her earliest memories that morning. She was given a pad of paper and a glass of water and then was shown to the large table in the center of the room and left alone.

The conference room was in the rear of the facility and had large windows on three sides. From a seated position at the table, Rose could view the entire office. She could see the front door and the back of the receptionist, the people coming in and leaving through the main entrance. She could observe the desks where the deputies sat, only a couple of them present, and she could view the side entrance, which was next to a small kitchen where the staff went in and out to grab a bite to eat or to get a drink from the vending machine.

Rose sat and watched the activity around her for a few minutes, procrastinating about what she'd been asked to do. With a sigh, she finally began writing all that had occurred from the moment she left the campground office to search for the late-night arrival until the sheriff had been called. She recorded every detail, as best as she could remember.

She wrote down how she drove around all the sites in the main area of the campground, how she ran into a few of the campers, and how she then followed the dog to the camper in the unused section of the grounds. She recorded the approximate times of each event.

She listed the model of the camper, the make of the truck, and how she had seen the small opening in the curtain, which led her to discover the destruction inside and the man lying on the floor. She wrote of how she used a rock to break the window and how the camper looked once she got inside.

She recorded that it appeared to her, based upon her professional opinion as a health-care provider, that the man was deceased. She noted that there were large bruises around his neck and that she'd found him beneath the table, lying under a sheet, and that it appeared as if he had been dead for more than a few hours.

She wrote for about fifteen minutes, as clearly and with as many details as she could remember, and then she stopped, put down the pen, and leaned back against the soft padded chair. Having worked in a hospital for more than twenty years, she knew how to deliver a thorough report, but since it had been almost a year since she had been required to write one, she found the task exhausting.

She decided to take a break and she stretched her arms above her head and yawned. Then she glanced up and around the office again. She saw the deputy who had brought her into the conference room sitting at his desk, eating a bag of chips. He was reading from a folder of papers.

She saw two women standing near the water fountain next to the kitchen. She thought they must be administrative workers, since they weren't wearing uniforms. They were chatting and drinking sodas. She had never seen them before. She looked around the office until she turned back to the front entrance and noticed a large man talking to the woman at the front reception area.

He was dark-skinned, standing very tall and dignified, and his hair, long and silk black, was tied in a ponytail that trailed down past his shoulders. He was wearing a dark suit, navy or black—Rose couldn't tell which—and he carried a briefcase, which he continued to hold while he talked, his long, thick fingers curled around the handle.

He stood at an angle in front of the desk, so that Rose saw only his profile, a long side view of a well-built, well-dressed stranger. He kept both arms at his sides, appearing very businesslike. He is certainly an eye-catcher, Rose thought.

And then, suddenly, while Rose sat watching him, as if she had called him, he turned and stared right at her through the conference room window. It was as if he knew she was in there, as if he had registered that she was studying him.

Rose quickly looked away, feeling as if she had been discovered or caught, and peered down at the pages on the table. She felt her face redden as she tried to appear as if she was reading over what she had written. She waited only a few seconds, hoping he had turned away, but when she glanced up again, the receptionist was on the phone and the man was gone.

At that moment, the conference door opened and in walked Sheriff Montgomery. The sudden entry startled her and she jumped.

"Well, so glad you decided to come by." He shut the door behind him and moved to the chair across from Rose without registering her surprise. "I thought you would be here before lunch. I got tired of waiting on you and ran some errands." He noticed the pad of paper and her pen. "Looks like they got you taken care of."

Rose looked around the station. The sheriff had entered from the side entrance and the tall, dark stranger was nowhere to be seen. The two women near the water fountain had returned to their desks.

"It took longer at the doctor's office than we thought." Then she faced the sheriff and confessed. "Actually, we had a little celebration at the Dairy Queen. Ms. Lou Ellen was given a clean bill of health."

"Well, that's dandy for you and your friend." He sat down and picked up the pages Rose had finished.

"You done?" he asked, referring to her statement.

"Just about," she replied, shaking off the feeling of being caught. "I've gotten to the part where I broke the door and found the dead man."

"Right," he replied. "The unlawful entry."

"The good instinct," she quipped.

He raised his head to look her in the eyes. "Okay, Nurse Franklin," he said in a conciliatory tone. "A medical emergency."

She smiled. "Hey, did you find out who the guy is?" She stopped abruptly. "I mean was."

"Not yet," he replied. "But we did contact the police in Gallup, New Mexico, where the truck is registered. We should hear something by the end of the day, I imagine." He placed the written statement back in front of Rose.

"Finish this up and then bring it over to my office." He nodded with his chin to the far side of the station.

Rose peered behind her and saw the door to the corner office. She had not noticed the space before. She nodded and then asked, "Is there a large Native American population in West Memphis?" She was still thinking about the man she had just seen, wondering if he was local or was visiting.

"Not a population at all," he responded. "Not since the Europeans arrived in the 1400s. The Mississippi valley used to be home to a great many Indian tribes," he noted, "but that all changed once Columbus and those other celebrated explorers found the shores of these United States."

Rose considered the sheriff's words. She realized she knew only very little about the Indians in the southeastern part of the country. The stranger at the reception desk still had her interest.

"Are there any groups still around here?" she asked,

wondering if the man she had seen and the dead camper were related in any way.

"Not really organized," he replied. "Even though we're west of the Mississippi, which is where they were all sent at the time of the Indian Removal Act, they marched them on past us into Oklahoma. So there are not too many tribes around here. It's strange that they've all gone, since geographically we aren't too far from Poverty Point and the Hopewell societies."

Rose was puzzled.

"You never heard of Poverty Point?" he asked. Then he waved his hand in front of himself. "I forget that most folks don't know the Indians' story in this part of the country. It's not usually discussed in the history books."

He sat forward in his chair. "I started reading about the cultures after I found an old fossil when I was hunting near Hot Springs. It turned out to be a carving, a shell gorget with a strange figure on it. I took it to the museum director at the state capital and he told me it was from around 1300, a ceremonial piece from the early tribes somewhere in the Southeast, maybe Mississippi. Anyway, it got me interested in that part of history. Turns out that the river used to be a big gathering spot for Indians all across the country."

He stopped and took a deep breath, realizing he was more than likely boring Rose. "It's a hobby for me."

Rose thought about the bracelet, how Sheriff Montgomery could probably explain a lot about it, that it might even generate some warm feelings between them, but then she remembered that she had not told him about it when he asked her at the murder scene if she had any other information. She hadn't included it in her statement. She decided not to say anything about it, since she worried that telling him now might ultimately make things worse.

"You suddenly interested in Indian history because of the dead man?" he asked, pulling Rose from her thoughts.

"Sure," she said. "And then I just saw a guy at your front desk, not more than ten minutes ago. He was definitely Indian," she said. "I just wondered where he might have been from, if he might have known the deceased."

Sheriff Montgomery turned to look at the front entry. He turned back to Rose. "Wouldn't know," he said. "I came in from the side, so I haven't checked my messages." He focused again on the uncompleted pages in front of Rose.

"Well, finish this up and drop it on my desk on your way out," he said as he stood up from his chair. "That will be all we need from you for now. I'll be over at Shady Grove again tomorrow morning to check things out again."

He moved to the conference room door, then turned around. "You're not going to involve yourself any further in this, are you?" he asked, giving her a suspicious look.

"Not unless I uncover another medical emergency," she replied. She waited a moment, then smiled innocently.

The sheriff made a huffing noise and shook his head. "I'm asking you nicely, Rose. Stay out of my investigation." Then he turned and walked out of the conference room.

Rose watched him as he went to the front desk and spoke to the receptionist. He took a handful of notes, which Rose assumed were his messages, and then headed into his office. She took a drink of water and finished her report.

SEVEN

Rose left the sheriff's office and headed straight to the library. She planned to go to the history section to search for a book that could help her decipher the symbols on the dead man's bracelet. She thought Ms. Lou Ellen had given her good advice about identifying them, but instead of drawing the symbols on a piece of paper and taking that to the library, she'd just decided to take the piece of jewelry along with her. She figured that she would be able to find a private place where no one would see her and where she could do the research without being discovered.

Having visited the library a few times during her stay in West Memphis, she knew that on a Tuesday afternoon the place would be mostly unoccupied, and she was right. The library was empty of people except for an older woman who appeared to be studying recipes from magazines, two teenaged boys at the computers, a young woman with a small child in the children's section, and two librarians. One of them was leaving when Rose walked in.

The younger woman, the librarian Rose had seen in the building before, held open the door, offering a polite greeting to Rose and waving good-bye to the woman standing behind the desk. This one, a round woman of middle age, was only vaguely familiar to Rose. She was busy on the phone when Rose stepped to the desk to ask her a question.

She dropped the receiver by her chin and pointed Rose to the reference section when she asked the location of books on Native American tribes.

The librarian was patiently giving information about an upcoming seminar that the library was offering, some sort of job fair or career counseling. Rose heard part of the conversation but quit paying attention when she found her way to the sought-after stacks.

Rose grabbed a couple of books from a shelf and then walked to a long table at the rear of the library. It was positioned against a wall, with chairs arranged around it. There were shelves of books on one side, and from where she sat, her back against the far wall, she was facing only a narrow hallway that led to a rear entrance. She glanced around, and, seeing no one around, decided this was a good place where she could do her work without being noticed.

She had taken a few extra pieces of paper from the pad she had been given when she made her statement for Sheriff Montgomery. And when she took these out of her purse, along with a pen, she wondered if she should have asked the deputy before she took them.

Too late, she thought to herself, and placed them in front of her. She pushed her purse under the table and then, just to be safe, reached inside her coat pocket and touched the bracelet. She chose to keep the piece of jewelry out of sight. She removed her jacket, however, since it was warm in the library, and hung it on the back of her chair.

Once she'd located the reference section, she found that there were not many books that she considered would be helpful. She hadn't been specific with the librarian when she'd asked for assistance, because the woman had been preoccupied with the person on the phone and because she didn't want to give any clues about why she was there. She had only requested information about southeastern Indian tribes, hoping she could find what she was looking for once she was directed to the proper section.

She'd found an encyclopedia of North American Indian tribes and a large book about Indian history published by Reader's Digest. She opened up the encyclopedia first and searched for anything resembling what she had seen on the jewelry. She looked up the tribes from New Mexico as well as tribes around the Mississippi River.

She began to read. She took in the information before her, soon realizing that she had never known that there were so many different tribes of Indians in America, nor had she ever really heard the harsh stories of massacre and eradication that happened to so many once the Europeans arrived.

Like most everyone else, Rose held a Hollywood version of native people. First, there was the savage image of Indians chasing the pioneers, stealing the women, and then there was the mythical one, the image of a people deeply connected to the earth, the image that the New Agers seemed particularly interested in. Even though she had read sympathetic accounts, those that spoke of the stories of the smallpox blankets and the introduction of alcohol, Rose had never read the stories of the complete destruction of tribes, the vast genocide that had occurred in this country.

After reading a few chapters, she closed the first book and opened the next one. There was only more of the same: epidemics, enslavement, death, and forced removal. She stopped reading and reached inside her pocket and pulled out the bracelet. She held it in her hands, thinking about the old man, about his history, his family, about dying alone in a strange place, about his violent end and how it now seemed to resemble the violent ends of so many of his ancestors.

She searched the book again, then turned to the index and searched for the word *symbols*. She flipped to the pages listed and found an entire section discussing symbols of different tribes. These symbols, she discovered, had been carved on cave and canyon walls, near the villages and pueblos, and along migration routes. They had been recorded and deciphered by scores of anthropologists and other persons interested in petroglyphs. She found some of the ones Ms. Lou Ellen had mentioned, as well as a couple that she recognized from the bracelet.

One of the symbols, the two circles, one inside the other, she learned, was a sign for the sun. The small square, completely dark inside, was considered to be a sign of death. The parallel lines had been correctly identified by Ms. Lou Ellen. According to the book Rose read, this was a sign for a trail or a map. She pulled the bracelet from her pocket and studied it again. Three other symbols remained that she hadn't found.

There was one with a parallel set of dotted lines running vertically, connected with small horizontal lines. There was a circle with half of it darkened, the other half bearing a few dots. Finally, there was one with several characters carved, with lines above the tops of them. Rose inspected the bracelet and then placed it back in her pocket. She wrote down the symbols that she had identified.

"We don't have a copier for the public. Well, we had one, but it's broken."

Rose glanced up from her research when she heard the librarian talking. It was the same woman who had guided her to the reference section. She recognized her voice from the telephone conversation.

"You can try the post office," the woman added. "They've got one that uses credit cards."

"And where is your post office?" a man asked, and the voice caught Rose's attention. It was deep, with a slowed articulation of words. It wasn't exactly familiar, but it was interesting. She listened.

"It's on the next corner," the librarian told him. Then there was a pause. Rose figured the librarian was pointing the post office out to the stranger, who was probably looking down the street in the direction of the building with a public copier.

"Where are you from?" the woman asked, appearing to make an effort to sound cheerful and hospitable instead of nosy, which was how Rose thought the line of questioning was more clearly interpreted.

"Louisiana," the man replied hesitantly. "Natchez," he added softly. "Natchez, Louisiana."

"Oh, Natchez," the woman responded, as if he had just named her hometown and he was some long-lost cousin. "My neighbor is from Natchez."

Rose rolled her eyes. She could tell from the silence that the stranger probably wished he hadn't stopped in the library for assistance.

"Isn't that south from here, straight down the river?" she asked even more cheerfully than before.

There was a pause. Rose listened.

"You're thinking of Natchez, Mississippi," he replied, his tone flat and bored.

"There's two Natchezes?" the librarian asked, drawing out the city's name into more than a few syllables.

"Yes, ma'am," the man replied.

"Well, I need to find out which Natchez she's from. Maybe she hails from Louisiana, too."

There was another moment of silence.

"Okay, thank you," the man said.

"Shug," the woman said sweetly and in more of a hushed tone, though everyone in the library could certainly hear her, "just give me what you need copied and I'll do it in the office for you."

Rose thought that the librarian was probably trying to make up for her geographical blunder. By this time, she had quit researching and was listening intently.

"No," the man replied curtly, then added, "I will take care of it."

"Really, the chief librarian is gone today. He's in Little Rock, trying to get us more money." The librarian's voice got softer but remained audible. "We've overspent the budget," she said. "It's the computers."

"I'll just go to the post office."

Rose leaned forward to hear more clearly.

"Honey, I don't mind. Just give me your papers and I'll do it for you." She sounded insistent.

"No" came the stern reply. And with that, Rose heard a shuffle and then the library door opened and closed.

She got up from her seat at the back table and walked around the corner to see the man, whose voice she had found so interesting, departing.

"Well, I was only trying to be helpful," the librarian said in a defensive tone once she noticed that Rose had stepped near her.

Rose offered no reply. She peered out the door, watching the stranger as he headed down the side-walk.

"Some people just have no manners," the librarian added, stacking books on the cart beside her. Her lips were pulled in a straight, tight line and her face was flushed. "I was just trying to be helpful," she said again. "But I guess it's true: Some people you just can't help."

"Maybe he didn't want to have you looking at his papers," Rose replied, thinking it was a simple obser-vation. She had not considered that the woman might take it as an insult.

The librarian loaded a few more books on the cart.

Rose turned toward the sidewalk and noticed the ponytail hanging down the man's back, the tall, dark manner of his figure. She recognized immediately that he was the same stranger she had seen in the sheriff's office.

He halted his pace, stopped. Rose hurried behind the shelves before she could see him pivot around and peer in her direction.

"Hon," the chatty librarian said to Rose, noticing her quick move behind the shelves next to the desk.

"Is there something else I can help you with?"

Her tone was not so cheerful. She was facing Rose and had not seen the man turn and look back.

"Uh, I'm fine," Rose said as she peeked around the corner to make sure that the stranger was now gone. She blew out a breath.

"Well, you could tell me if there are any other history books you might have." She slid her hands down the front of her pants, then folded them across her chest, then dropped them by her sides. It was nervous behavior, and the librarian paid attention to it.

She studied Rose for a minute, putting down the books she held in her hands. "Do you have a library card?" she asked suspiciously.

"A what?" Rose asked.

"A library card," she said again. "You'll need a library card if you want to check anything out." The librarian narrowed her eyes at Rose.

"I'm not really from here," Rose said, feeling like she was suddenly being reprimanded. Even though she had been in the library at West Memphis before, she had not taken the time to register or to get a card. Any book she had wanted to read, Thomas or Ms. Lou Ellen had checked out for her, using their library cards.

"I don't plan to check anything out, but I can look at your books here, can't I?" she asked. "I mean, without a library card?"

The librarian hesitated. Clearly, she could not stop a visitor from studying in the county building.

"There's a section behind the magazines about local history. Maybe there will be something for you to browse through." She paused and then added sharply, "While you visit."

Rose gave her a broad fake smile and walked over to the section the librarian had mentioned. She found lots of books about the river and about the Civil War, about agriculture and state politics. She flipped through some of them, finding nothing of interest.

After searching the entire area that had been recommended to her, she soon learned that there were no books about Native Americans. She glanced across all the shelves in the history area and then returned to the table where she had been sitting and working. She did not notice right away that anything was different.

She sat in the chair and glanced down, aware that the pages in the book she had been reading appeared to be turned to a different section than the one she had been studying. She thought she remembered what she had been reading when she had walked away, but she figured at first that maybe a breeze coming from the vents around her had blown across the book and turned the pages.

Then she realized that her ink pen was no longer inside the large reference guide but was now positioned next to her paper, which also seemed to have been disturbed. What had previously been five or six sheets stacked on top of one another were now scattered on top of the desk. Again, Rose considered air from a vent, but she searched around and didn't see any vents near where she was seated and she felt no draft around her.

Then she leaned against the chair and, without really thinking, stuck her hand in the pocket of her coat, which she had left hanging there. And that was when she knew someone had been there. The bracelet was gone.

She reached into the other pocket. It had only her keys in it. She jumped up and glanced around her seat, across the table, under the books and her paper. Her purse was still there, her wallet still inside. Nevertheless, it was obvious to her what had happened. Somebody had reached inside her jacket and stolen the bracelet.

She ran to the front desk. The librarian was not there. Rose assumed she was in the rear office somewhere, but she couldn't see anyone behind the glass partition. She spun around to see who was still present in the library. She saw the young woman with the child, the two teenaged boys at the computers. The older woman was gone from the magazine section, but Rose spotted her returning from the rest room. Like the others in the library, the woman acted as if nothing out of the ordinary had occurred.

Rose faced back toward the desk and the office. "Excuse me," she said loudly.

The two teenagers looked up from the computers. The women heard her, as well, but Rose didn't care if she was making too much noise.

"Hello," she said, showing a fair amount of concern

in her voice. "Are you still here?" she asked, leaning against the counter, trying to gain the attention of the librarian.

There was no reply. The others in the library only stared at her. Rose hurried around the desk and walked into the office. She saw a doorway leading behind the office. She headed toward it. She turned the corner and barreled right into the librarian.

"Good heavens!" the woman screamed. She backed away from Rose, trying to gain her composure. Then she quickly yelled, "You can't be in here!" She was obviously rattled by the surprising presence.

Rose peered behind the woman and saw a rear entrance and a staff bathroom. Both doors were standing open.

"Did you see anybody else in here?" she asked. She was certainly not concerned about trespassing in the staff quarters.

"What?" the woman asked. Now, no longer startled, she stepped closer to Rose. "I've been in the office." She stopped speaking, assessing the situation, "Wait, I told you that you can't be back here. This is for employees only." And she placed her fists on her hips. "Why are you here?" she asked Rose.

"Somebody stole—" She stopped and thought better of what she was saying. "I've lost something and I needed to know if you've seen anybody else come in the library." She spoke in an agitated tone.

The librarian took in a breath and then blew it out slowly. She glanced above Rose's head and saw the older woman from the magazine section standing at the front desk. She raised her chin in her direction and then moved around Rose.

"You need to return to the desk. I will not answer your questions in this hallway." And she jerked her head up and down and headed toward the side door to the office.

She held open the door while Rose walked through. Then she closed the door behind them. Rose hurried through the other door and around the desk. She glanced over and saw the woman who had been reading the magazines waiting for assistance. It was clear to Rose that the librarian was not going to be helpful to her. In fact, Rose thought that the librarian could possibly even make things worse, so she returned to the table where she had been working.

She checked everything again. She retraced all of her steps, thinking that maybe she had put the bracelet in her pants pocket and that it had dropped out when she went to see the stranger the librarian had been talking to.

She walked through the stacks, searching to see if there was anyone new in the library who might have entered when she wasn't watching. She stood behind the computers and watched the two boys who were playing games and who seemed not at all interested in the woman staring at them.

She went around to the children's section, deciding finally that there was nothing odd about the woman reading to her child. And the older woman, who had gathered her things and was standing at the front desk talking to the librarian, seemed completely harmless.

Rose noticed that both of the women had turned and were watching her as she rambled about, trying to figure out what had happened to the bracelet. They turned around and began to whisper to each other, but Rose didn't care if they were talking about her. All she could think about was the piece of jewelry that she had taken and that had now been taken from her.

She headed to her place at the table and sat down. She leaned forward in the chair, searching again under the table and around where she had been sitting. She lifted the books from the desk, shuffled the papers. There was still nothing. She glanced around the library again, this time studying the rear entry, which was straight down the aisle from where she was sitting. The leaves of a plant next to the door were swaying from side to side, as if the door had only recently been opened and closed.

Rose watched the plant until it stopped moving, and when she sat back, her arms hanging at her sides, she reached into the pocket of her jacket again and wrapped her fingers around the bracelet. She understood as she held it in her hand that in the short time she had run around the library trying to recover the jewelry, it had been returned.

EIGHT

Well, what do you mean it was stolen?" Ms. Lou Ellen was staring at the bracelet the younger woman had placed on her kitchen table. She poured Rose a cup of tea and sat down across from her. Her new companion, the three-legged dog, lay at her feet under the table.

"It was gone," Rose replied. She had left the library and driven straight to Shady Grove. Mary was in the office, working on reservations, so Rose had stopped at Ms. Lou Ellen's to talk to her. She was, after all, the only one who knew that Rose had taken the jewelry.

"But dear, it's right here," she said calmly.

"I know. That's what's so weird. He stole it and then he returned it." She sounded exasperated.

"Who, dear?" The older woman sipped from her cup of tea.

"The tall, dark stranger," Rose replied. "The same one I saw at the sheriff's office. He followed me to the library and he sneaked in and stole the bracelet, and then he put it back in my pocket."

Ms. Lou Ellen leaned in toward her friend. "Are you getting enough rest?" she asked in a concerned tone. "You know, most adults do not get enough sleep. An average woman needs at least eight hours a night. And an above-average woman, which I believe

79

includes the likes of both you and me"—she pointed first at herself, then at Rose—"needs nine." She reached up and squeezed the younger woman on the arm. "Do you get nine hours of sleep, dear?"

Rose shook her head. "I know, it sounds crazy." She placed her elbows on the table and then dropped her chin in her hands.

"How did he know I had the bracelet? Why would he take it for only a minute? Who is he and why has he shown up now?" She sat slumped in her chair.

"Drink your tea, Rose. It has chamomile in it. It will help soothe your nerves."

Rose took her cup of tea and drank a few sips. Then she returned the cup to the saucer and picked up the bracelet to examine it again. She slid her legs under the table, disturbing the dog. He yelped and moved closer to the older woman's feet.

"Sorry, Mr. Perkins," Rose said to the dog when she realized that she had kicked him.

"Call him Lester Earl," Ms. Lou Ellen said. "He never liked formalities." Then she reached down and petted the dog on the head. "Except from his wife. He liked it when I called him 'mister.' " She winked at Rose.

The younger woman continued. "I just know that when I returned to the library table and reached in my pocket, the bracelet was not there. And then after I ran around searching for it and got back and felt for it again, it was there." Rose was still sorting through the events that had occurred only a short time earlier.

"Well, what were you doing before you realized that it was missing?" Ms. Lou Ellen asked. "Go over it all again with me."

"I got a couple of books from the reference section and then I found a table in the back, a table where I was sure no one could see me. When I first sat down, I started reading."

Rose considered her activity at the library. She suddenly recalled some of the facts that she had learned. "Did you know that there were people living here in the Mississippi valley at the same time Solomon was the king of Israel? Or that there was a place in northeastern Louisiana called Poverty Point, where sometime around the year 1500 B.C. it was probably the biggest and most prosperous place in North America?" Rose paused.

Ms. Lou Ellen nodded. "The place with the bird mound," she replied.

Rose seemed surprised.

"That would be from my last husband, the history professor."

The dog whined from beneath the table.

"Oh Lester, he was long after you." And she petted the dog again. "Anyway, I'm sorry for interrupting. Continue, dear."

"Okay, so I was reading from the books I had taken," she said, then became sidetracked again. "We did some pretty horrible things to the Indians when we got here."

Ms. Lou Ellen nodded knowingly.

"Anyway, I heard the librarian talking to a man, and for some reason I was intrigued by his voice, so I started listening to their conversation." She paused.

The older woman raised her eyebrows, "Eavesdropping," she said in a whisper. She placed her index finger to her lips.

"Yes, I was eavesdropping," Rose confessed. "I got up to see the Indian guy and I watched him walk away. I recognized him from before, when I had seen him at the sheriff's office."

"The tall, dark stranger," Ms. Lou Ellen inserted.

"Right. Then the librarian, who is quite an unlikable person, by the way—"

"Miss Stokely," Ms. Lou Ellen said, interrupting. "She's still mad because the love of her life left her at the altar." She took a sip of her tea and then whispered, "He left town with her sister." She leaned in toward Rose. "And there was poor Miss Stokely, plump as a pea, dressed up in a long white gown with tiny white pearls, the thin veil covering her shame, standing in a church filled with geraniums." Ms. Lou Ellen folded her hands and gently placed them on the table. "That in itself was reason to leave her."

"Because she was plump?" Rose asked, not following.

"For heaven's sake, no, because of the plants," the older woman replied. "Who ever heard of geraniums as a wedding flower? That marriage was doomed the moment she decided to use her houseplants as decoration."

"Well, that would explain her surly behavior." Rose smiled and drank the last of her tea. "So, back to the story," she continued. "I tried to find some more books but didn't see any, and then I returned to the table. That's when I discovered that the pages were turned in the book I had been reading, that my pen was in a different place, and that the bracelet was gone."

"How long had you been absent from your belongings?" Ms. Lou Ellen asked.

"Ten or fifteen minutes at the most," Rose replied.

There was a pause as Ms. Lou Ellen considered what her friend had told her.

"Maybe it slipped through your fingers the first time. Maybe you just thought it was gone." She added some more water to her tea.

"It was gone," Rose said confidently.

"Rose dear, haven't you ever searched for something over and over, around every inch of your house, and then come across it right where you were sure you had already looked?"

Rose leaned back against her chair. She stared up at the ceiling. "Yes," she said hesitantly, "of course." She sat up and faced her friend.

"Well, maybe that's all it was," Ms. Lou Ellen said reassuringly.

Rose considered the idea but didn't seem to believe it.

"Or, it could be something else." Ms. Lou Ellen drummed her fingers on the table. She waited a minute and then resumed speaking. "Maybe it was your guilt washing over you for stealing the evidence from the crime scene." She began to explore her newest assessment. Rose listened, though she bore a puzzled look on her face.

"Maybe since you had just returned from Sheriff Montgomery, knowing that you had engaged in deceit and the looting of a dead man, and then, having sat down to read those ghastly accounts of our atrocities against the native peoples, you aligned yourself with the evil forces at work in the world from the beginning of time and it suddenly created the illusion in your mind of having been offended yourself." She seemed pleased with her emerging analysis of what had happened to her friend.

"Or perhaps you were so enveloped in your state of monkey business that your fingers became sensory-dysfunctional, paralyzed, if you will, unable to decipher the shape and feel of the pilfered piece of evidence that remains in your possession."

Ms. Lou Ellen pounded a fist on the table, startling both Rose and the dog. She was a lawyer at the judge's desk, now making her case with great fervor.

"You could not recognize the thick silver band because your soul had been compromised by your actions. And even on a deeper level, you were sub-consciously cloaked from the consequence of your thievery because you did not want to touch the sub-stantiation of your connection to the immoral deeds of our ancestors who arrived on the shores of this fair land and proceeded to steal from and lie to those who had already discovered America."

She stopped and then ended with a great depth of emotion. "The earliest settlers, the Indians."

The older woman, having finished her speech, clasped her hands together in front of her chest, leaned back against her chair, closed her eyes, and exhaled a long, noisy breath. She had wrapped her closing argument and was now basking in the light of her conclusion.

Rose was unsure of how to respond. There was an awkward silence.

"Then again, dear," Ms. Lou Ellen said as she sat up and faced her friend, "perhaps you just stuck your hand in the wrong pocket." She smiled and nodded at Rose, then got up from her seat and walked over to the sink, placing her cup under the faucet.

"Well, it appears as if we have company," she said, now speaking in a light, cheerful tone. She was standing in front of the kitchen window, which faced the campground office.

Rose seemed baffled, first by her friend's line of thinking and her explanation for what had occurred at the library and second by the quick change of topic. She shook her head, as if that would help clear her mind.

"Who do we know who drives a long gold Cadillac bearing North Carolina plates?"

Ms. Lou Ellen had retrieved her pair of opera

glasses from the shelf beside the sink and was investigating the new arrival.

As soon as she heard "gold Cadillac," Rose jumped up from the table, frightening Lester Earl, and ran to the window to stand beside her friend. The dog howled and hobbled to the corner of the room.

"I can't believe it," Rose said in a hushed voice as she watched a man step out from the driver's side, a man she clearly recognized, a man who had always claimed that when he turned forty he was buying himself a gold Cadillac and driving across the country.

There was a moment in which she felt almost happy to see her ex-husband, but as soon as the passenger door opened and the long legs of the woman she assumed was his new wife emerged, the hint of pleasure was dulled.

NINE

How do I look?" Rose asked her friend anxiously. She began to smooth down her blouse and then quickly searched around the room for a mirror.

"Just like yourself," Ms. Lou Ellen replied, still unsure of who had just driven up to the campground. She turned to the younger woman and was examining her through the opera glasses. Rose was magnified. "Only a whole lot bigger," she added.

"I can't believe he's here," Rose said fretfully, still watching out the window.

"And just who is this 'he'?" Ms. Lou Ellen asked.

"Rip," Rose replied, sounding out of breath, "My ex-husband."

Ms. Lou Ellen turned to the dog resting under the table. "Was there some convention you fellows attended that suggested you visit previous wives?" she asked her new companion. "Did you decide that it would be more of an advantage if all of the ex-husbands of the women at Shady Grove showed up at once?"

The dog sat up as if he had been called. Ms. Lou Ellen spun back to the window and to the scene that was taking place just outside her door.

The man stood and stretched; then he hurried to the passenger door, opening it wide. He bent down and gave the woman inside his hand. Out came a tall, thin, tan, very young, very blond woman. He nervously closed the door behind her as she glanced around at her new surroundings. They walked up the steps and into the office.

"And he brought her," Rose cried. "Her!" she said again. "What on earth is he thinking?"

Ms. Lou Ellen followed them with her opera glasses. "That somehow spending time with a younger woman will help him forget the bald spot on the back of his head and the fact that his penis has shrunk."

The dog made a yelping noise and moved from the

corner of the kitchen to the rear bedroom. Ms. Lou Ellen watched her new pet as he hurried away, his tail curled beneath his one rear leg.

"Oh, I apologize, dear," she called out to the departing dog. "Lester Earl," she shouted, "I'm sorry. I did promise I wouldn't mention your indiscretion again." She waited. The dog did not return.

"Oh well," she said to Rose as she leaned forward, straining her neck to follow the couple as they walked up the steps to the office. "The truth does hurt, even when spoken to a dog."

Rose began to panic. "What should I do?" she asked. "I mean, should I try to get to my car or just hide in here?"

At that moment, the couple walked back out to the porch of the office, Mary standing between them. The campground manager pointed to the small cabin where the two women were staring out of the window. Rose immediately hit the floor when she realized that they were now peering in her direction.

"Quick, get down here," Rose said to her friend, pulling on her sweater.

Ms. Lou Ellen did not move, but, rather, braced herself at the sink. "Darling, the last time I got on my knees was during one of Lucas's prayer meetings at the church. I love my daughter's husband, but I don't go to his prayer meetings anymore because I have known for a very long time now that I can talk to the Good Lord just fine sitting in a chair."

She cleared her throat. "My dear, I don't drop down

unless I'm quite sure I will get back up. Besides, I've only very recently been released from my doctor's care." She leaned toward Rose. "A broken hip," she added, pointing to her right side. "It is not recommended for me to squat."

Then she faced the window again. "Well, they are now about forty yards away, so you better decide if you're running for cover in the back with the guilty dog or if you're going to stand up like a woman and face this man and his middle-aged mistake."

"I don't know what to do," Rose stammered. "Tell me what to do," she said, pleading with her friend.

"Get up, drink a few swallows of water, throw some on your face and get ahold of yourself," Ms. Lou Ellen replied in a commanding voice. She poured a glass of water and handed it to Rose, who remained seated on the floor.

The couple was now walking up the cabin steps.

"Tell them I'm not here," Rose said, waving off the water.

She began crawling toward the rear of the house. Ms. Lou Ellen watched with a disapproving look on her face.

There was a knock. Rose froze just beside the table. Ms. Lou Ellen made a huffing noise, walked over to the front entrance, and opened the door wide enough for the couple to see Rose hiding under the table.

"It fell under the chair," the older woman said to her friend, providing an explanation as to why the other woman was down on all fours on the floor. "Keep searching, I'm sure it's there somewhere." Then she faced the curious man and woman standing at her door.

"Well, hello there," she said in her most delicate manner.

She wore a huge smile across her face. "Rose dear," she said as if she were surprised, "we have guests."

She stood away from the door and Rose turned to look. She remained on her hands and knees for only a second and then quickly jumped to her feet.

"Rip, hello," she said, her voice filled with just a bit too much cheer. "What a surprise to see you here," she added, walking toward the couple. She stood beside Ms. Lou Ellen.

She extended her hand. Rip reached out and shook it. The moment was awkward for all of them.

"Did you find it, dear?" Ms. Lou Ellen asked, still trying to cover the charade.

"What?" Rose asked.

"It," Ms. Lou Ellen replied quickly.

"Oh, right, yes, it was in my pocket," she said, trying to think of the best way to respond.

"Of course it was," the older woman replied. "That's where it's been the entire time." She smiled and nodded, reminding Rose of their earlier conversation.

Ms. Lou Ellen faced Rip and the woman with him. "Would you like to come in?" she asked.

Rose immediately stood between Ms. Lou Ellen and the couple, blocking them from getting through the door.

"I think we'll just go outside and talk," she said as she walked past them to the front porch.

"Ah, okay," Rip said. "Nice to meet you," he said to Ms. Lou Ellen.

"But we didn't," she responded.

The man seemed surprised. Rose blew out a breath.

"Meet," the older woman explained.

"Oh, right," he responded. "I'm Rip Griffith. This is my wife, Victoria."

Rose felt a sudden pain in the center of her chest at the introduction. She swayed briefly but caught herself before anyone else noticed.

"Pleased to meet you," the young wife added.

"Lou Ellen Johnston," the older woman said casually, holding out her hand. Rip reached for it and shook it. Then she added, "Rose has become my dearest friend." She glanced over at the woman now holding on to the banister at the front steps. When she caught Rose's eye, she winked.

It immediately eased the situation for the middle-aged nurse, the ex-wife of Rip Griffith. She smiled at Ms. Lou Ellen and felt the sting slighten and then disappear.

"Great," Rip responded. "Thank you, then," he said, and slid his arm around Victoria.

The two of them followed Rose as she walked toward the row of picnic tables just beside the office.

"What are you doing here?" she asked as she sat down at the far side of the tables.

He sat down across from her. The younger woman

seemed either bored or uncomfortable. Rose couldn't tell which.

"Honey, I think I'll walk around while the two of you talk," Victoria said. She grinned at Rose and flipped her long blond hair with the back of her hand. "Good to see you again," she said to Rose, then kissed her new husband on the cheek.

"Okay, right," Rip said, holding his wife by the arm as she bent over him.

Rose quickly turned away. "Stay on the path," she said to Victoria, who peered up at her with a perplexed look. "Snakes," she added, knowing it was way too soon in the season for the copperheads or even the harmless black or garden variety to be out around the riverbanks. "They're mean when you step on them this early." She meant to frighten the young woman, and it did just that.

Victoria quickly jumped to the gravel road. She glanced around nervously and then started walking toward the river.

Rip watched his wife; then he faced Rose. "There are no snakes," he said, recognizing what she was doing. He smiled at her.

"From what I see, a few just crawled out from under some rock." She surprised herself with her sarcasm. It wasn't like her to be so confrontational.

Rip understood her sentiment. It startled him, too. He chose not to respond to her statement.

"So, how are you, Rose?" he asked, trying to sound as sincere as possible.

"I'm doing just fine," she replied. "You're obviously doing well." She was staring at the Cadillac still parked in front of the office. She glimpsed over to her friend's cabin and saw the older woman watching from the bedroom window. She was still using her opera glasses and the dog was beside her. Ms. Lou Ellen waved in Rose's direction.

"Oh, the car." He swung around to look at his most recent purchase, then turned back to face Rose. "The business had a good quarter."

Rose nodded without a reply. She sighed, waiting for her ex-husband to explain why he had suddenly arrived in West Memphis, Arkansas, from Rocky Mount, North Carolina.

"I came here because I needed to talk to you," he said, realizing there wasn't going to be any more small talk and that she was waiting for the reason for his surprise visit. He hesitated, took a breath, placed both of his hands on the table between them.

Rose studied her ex-husband. She thought he was smaller somehow than she remembered. And Ms. Lou Ellen was right: He was balding. Both the sides and the top of his head showed signs of thinning hair. She considered briefly the other part of her friend's observation but decided to let that thought go. She softened.

"What is it, Rip?" she asked.

"It's your father, the captain," he said quietly.

Rose waited for more.

"He's gotten a lot worse." Rip seemed genuinely concerned.

Rose didn't reply. She knew when she left North Carolina several months earlier that she was leaving a man in his last season of life. She knew from her work as a nurse, from reading the nursing home reports, from his appearance the week she left, that he would not last much longer.

She had known that not being present at his time of death was certainly a possibility when she chose to move out of her hometown. The news was not a shock to her, but that fact that her ex-husband was the one bringing it to her was a surprise.

"Why didn't Dennis call?" she asked, referring to her brother, knowing that his relationship with their father was no better than hers.

Capt. Morris Burns had been abusive to his children, a mean and nasty drunk. Neither Rose nor Dennis felt as if they owed their father anything.

"He said that you made the right decision to leave and that he wasn't going to bring you back for the old man." Rip appeared embarrassed to be speaking so intimately of a family to which he was no longer connected.

Rose nodded. Her brother had a good heart and they loved each other as well as they were able, having survived the childhoods that they'd had. They had managed a relationship as adults in spite of the fact that he had left home at an early age and she had had to fend for herself. She had been angry with him for years and he had felt guilty about it for just as many. They did not speak for a long time, but when she married and by the time his children were born, Rose and Dennis had become brother and sister again.

The sun was lowering as the afternoon was quickly fading. Although it had warmed up a few hours prior to the visit of her ex-husband, the temperature had dropped again and Rose was now chilled without her jacket. She had left it at Ms. Lou Ellen's. She ran her hands up and down her arms.

"Here," Rip said, yanking off his sweatshirt and handing it to his ex-wife. "I don't need it."

Rose took the shirt and wrapped it around her arms. "Thank you," she said softly.

They sat in silence for a while. They both stared across the campground out to the river. Two ducks flew over their heads and landed in the small pond beside them. Rose watched as the two of them settled on the water, the surface rippling and then growing still.

"So, why did you come here to tell me this?" Rose asked. "Why didn't you just call or write a letter?"

Rip didn't answer at first; then he shrugged his shoulders. "I told you I always wanted to drive across the country. It's kind of a late honeymoon for us," he said, referring to himself and Victoria.

Rose turned away. She did not appreciate hearing that she was just a stop on his vacation, especially since it was a vacation with his new wife.

"And because I wanted to see you, find out how you are." He waited. "Make sure you're okay," he added.

She nodded. "I'm good," she said, this time more honestly.

Since he seemed sincere, she decided to share more of her new life. "I like it here," she said as she glanced around, taking in the sights of her campground home. "I made some really good friends." She thought of telling him about Tom Sawyer, her new lover, but then refrained. "I work in the office. I walk a lot around the river and out past the new historical site." She pointed over to the memorial grounds with her chin, the grounds that she had helped make happen after she took part in solving the murder of Lawrence Franklin.

Rip looked in the direction she was indicating and nodded.

"I really do love the camper," she said, remembering how it was between them when they purchased it several years before the divorce.

"Yeah, I always knew you did," he replied.

Rose nodded. There was another pause.

"I just came because I know you, Rose. And as bad as your dad treated you, and I remember some of how bad it was . . ." He paused, looked down at the table, and then started again. "I stopped by to visit him one day. Victoria's grandmother is in the same place," he explained. "And I just went by his room. He was crying." Rip turned away. "I know it sounds crazy but it just seemed to me like he was trying to say he was sorry."

Rose felt her chest tighten even though she wasn't

sure exactly which part of what her ex-husband was saying was the most disturbing. She couldn't tell if she was more bothered hearing of her father's behavior or the fact she was hearing it from Rip.

"I just thought you should see him again before . . ." Rip hesitated. "I just thought you might need to hear what he was saying more than I did, that he needs to say it to you, to you and Dennis."

"I'd agree with you on that," she replied, and then asked, "Did he say he was sorry?"

Rip shook his head, signaling no.

Rose nodded. "So, you just assumed that his tears were evidence of his remorse?" she asked, feeling the defensive tone of her words.

She was angry that her father had only shown such emotion to him, her ex-husband, and not to her brother, not to her.

"There was just something about the way he looked at me," Rip said as a means of explaining how he'd come to his conclusion.

"A way he looked at you," Rose repeated.

She stared out across the Mississippi River and thought of the years that she had longed for such a look, any semblance, any possibility that he was really sorry for how he had treated her, all the times he had humiliated her in front of her friends, the blows across the face, the violent way he could explode over small things.

"It was no look," Rose said to Rip. "He's sick. He's got liver damage and Alzheimer's. That was no look," she said again. "That was just an old man whose body is shutting down."

Rip shrugged his shoulders, not sure of what else to say. "I guess you're right," he said.

They both heard a car approaching the office. They turned, to see a family emerge from a camper. A boy and girl took off running toward the river while the man and the woman walked onto the porch and into the office. It appeared that they were checking into Shady Grove.

"Well, I just felt like I should let you know," he responded.

"And I thank you for it," she said a little too quickly. Then she noticed the hurt in his eyes, the embarrassed way he suddenly held himself. She let down her guard.

"Look, Rip, I said my good-bye to my father when I left North Carolina. I don't hate him or despise him anymore. I'm done with all that. I made my peace," she acknowledged.

He didn't say anything at first, just recognized the truthfulness in his ex-wife's explanation. He watched the children run back to the camper and then inside the office to join their parents. He was hesitant to say anything else.

Finally, he replied, "I know, Rose, but he hasn't made his."

She glanced away from him, turning again to the Cadillac, the new arrivals, the four eyes still watching from the cabin.

She was going to say more to him, when suddenly there was a scream from the edge of the water at the far left end of the campground. Both Rose and Rip quickly stood up from their seats at the table, and when they did, they saw Victoria cleaving to the arm of one of the campers, Mr. Hinshaw.

Rose smiled when she realized he was holding up a rope, as if proving something to the younger woman. She was yelling and throwing her hands around wildly.

Rip rolled his eyes. "I guess I'll need to go and rescue her from the *snakes*." He shook his head. "Thank you, Rose, for traumatizing my wife."

Rose decided it was a good time to halt the conversation. She was glad for the distraction, even if it did come from a younger, prettier, slimmer, tanner Mrs. Griffith.

"It was my pleasure" was her response.

He stepped from behind the seat at the picnic table and walked around to his ex-wife. They stood facing each other for a moment until he stuck out his hand. Rose remembered the earlier greeting, the awkwardness behind it. And in a moment of tenderness, she pulled him into her.

They stood in an embrace until the screaming from down along the river had stopped.

TEN

W hy he come here now?" Mary asked Rose as the Cadillac pulled out of the campground. "He want you back?"

"Did you see the woman sitting next to him?" Rose replied.

"Ah, she be gone soon. She no woman to keep. She woman to show." Mary blew a loud breath through her lips.

"Maybe," Rose said softly, sorting through feelings of sadness and relief. Seeing Rip had brought up so many unexpected emotions for her.

She was nervous about seeing him, disappointed that he was still with the woman he had left the marriage for, a little angry that he had driven there to tell her about her father's condition, and lots of other things that she couldn't even articulate. But as she watched them driving away from Shady Grove, she was mostly just glad that he and his new wife were now gone.

There was a small cloud of dust that rose and fell as the car sped down the driveway and finally disappeared onto the road leading to the interstate.

The two women stood staring in that direction until the dirt settled and the long entryway into the campground was empty and undisturbed. They both then glanced up at the sky. The afternoon light was fading

and dusk was fast approaching. Rose suddenly realized that she was hungry and tired.

"Another strange day at Shady Grove," she said
with a sigh, recalling the murder, the incident at the
library, the bracelet she still had to return, the arrival
of her ex-husband.

She saw a few lights on a long barge skimming
across the river water. "Who knows what tomorrow
will bring?"

"More trouble," Mary replied, "if that dog stay
here." She was peering at the cabin across from the
office.

Ms. Lou Ellen was outside with her new pet. She
and the dog were standing next to a small grove of
trees. She turned and waved her handkerchief at her
two friends.

"Oh Mary," Rose said as they waved in return and
then walked up the steps. "He's harmless, and now he
doesn't have a place to stay." She held open the door.
"And he seems to make Ms. Lou Ellen happy.
Besides we could use a mascot here at Shady Grove,"
she added.

"Phsst," Mary replied. "Three-legged dog from
dead man's camper is no good mascot."

She walked through the door and stood behind the
counter. She began to sort through some papers on
her desk.

"I think he's sad and needs us," Rose replied, following Mary around to the desk.

"Maybe we should change our name," the office

manager responded. "No more Shady Grove, now Misfit Grove."

Rose smiled and considered her idea. "That may not be such a bad thought," she said.

The office manager seemed to be planning something else to say to her friend, but the phone suddenly began to ring. She shook her head, losing her train of thought, and then reached over and picked it up.

Rose sat down at the desk, watching her friend. She was warmer now than she had been earlier when she was sitting outside with Rip, because once the two of them were preparing to leave, she had gone to Ms. Lou Ellen's cabin and retrieved her jacket.

As Mary was talking on the phone, Rose felt inside the pocket to make sure the bracelet was secure. It was right where she had put it.

"Shady Grove," Mary said as a greeting.

"Ya, ya," she said while she nodded her head. She reached across the desk for a pad of paper and began writing something down, a message that the caller was giving. "Jacob Sunspeaker," she was repeating. "Okay," she said. "Tomorrow morning, okay." Then she placed the receiver in the cradle and wrote another note. Rose waited for her to explain.

"Man from FBI," she reported, telling her friend who it was on the phone. "Agent Loohan or Loowhan," she added. "I couldn't hear. He say dead man is from New Mexico, name Jacob Sunspeaker."

Rose nodded. She knew where he was from because of the license plate.

"They come first thing in the morning from some-where to search the truck and camper."

Mary returned the pen to the cup beside the pad of paper.

"Oh," Rose said. Then she added, "That's odd. I thought Sheriff Montgomery was going to come tomorrow and examine everything again. Did this guy say he was with the FBI?"

Mary studied her message. "He say he was an agent." She reflected on the conversation. "He sound like FBI." She sat down at her desk, seeming very confident of her assessment.

"How does the FBI sound?" Rose asked, uncertain of what her friend was implying.

"Short words, no small talk," she replied.

Then Rose asked the other question that had come to her mind after Mary's comment. "How do you know what they sound like?" she asked.

"My husband was not a very smart criminal," Mary replied, referring to Roger, the man who had brought her to Shady Grove. "For many years while he was in trouble, I learn how all lawmen sound."

Rose waited to hear more.

"Highway Patrol very courteous, call me Mrs. Mary Phillips. Deputies not too bright, talk too much about themselves. FBI always suspicious, say very little," she explained.

Rose nodded. She continued to be amazed at how much she was learning at the campground. Having been the daughter of a career police officer, she thought she knew everything about people working in the criminal justice system.

As she was pondering this information, both of the women heard motorcycles coming up the driveway, heading in the direction of the office. They smiled at each other and Rose said out loud what they both knew: "Rhonda and Lucas are back."

There were at least twelve or fifteen other bikers riding into the park with the couple. Mary and Rose watched as they pulled in, circled the campground, and then returned to the office. It was a kind of ritual with the Boyds. They always met up with their biker friends in town when they returned to West Memphis after one of their trips. After a brief reunion, the group always followed them into Shady Grove. It was a kind of Welcome Wagon greeting, a means of saying, We're home and we're making a lot of noise!

After a few minutes, Lucas and his wife, the owners of Shady Grove, entered the office. This time they had been gone for about three weeks, sailing near the Gulf of Mexico. They went there every year to help in a village somewhere on the east coast of Mexico. They built houses and did work on the school and the church. They also collected clothes and money for months and then took a boatload of supplies to the people at least twice a year.

"Well, little sisters," Lucas said as he greeted his two friends, giving each a kiss on the cheek.

Rhonda walked in behind her husband and hugged

Mary and Rose. They had both removed their helmets and appeared tired from their journey from where they sometimes docked their boat, down at the Arkansas-Louisiana state border. It was about a three-hour ride.

"I thought you wouldn't be back until the end of the month," Rose said, helping Rhonda take off her thick leather jacket. Rhonda's long red hair cascaded down along her shoulders. Rose had always thought the campground owner was beautiful, even though she was somewhat rough around the edges.

"Ah, little sister," Lucas replied, "the sheriff ended our mission work once again." Lucas took his wife's jacket and placed it on the coat tree by the table and then removed his and placed it there, as well.

"I tell him you are not to be disturbed," Mary said, sounding a bit irritated. She always tried hard to protect her employers and friends.

"Don't worry about it, Mary," Rhonda responded. "I wanted to see Mama anyway," she added.

"Did the doctor say everything was okay?" she asked Rose.

Rose nodded, remembering her early trip to the doctor's office. It seemed like days ago to her, given everything else that had happened. "She was released from his care this morning. However, she did request another month with her physical therapist."

"Leonard," both Lucas and Rhonda said at the same time. They knew Ms. Lou Ellen's appreciation for the young man who had been working with her for more than six months. They exchanged glances and Lucas winked at his wife.

"Well, bless the Lord," Ms. Lou Ellen's son-in-law added. "She does have a taste for men."

"Yeah, apparently even the reincarnated ones," Rose added.

Rhonda and Lucas seemed puzzled.

Mary made a hissing noise, understanding that Rose was referring to the dog. She waved her hand across her face.

Rhonda started to ask for an explanation but then proceeded to question them about the murder and what had happened that day at Shady Grove.

Rose reported everything to the couple. She told them about finding the man earlier in the day, how he had apparently been strangled, the destruction in his trailer, and how he had traveled alone with the three-legged dog that was now staying in the cabin next door. After she gave them all the information she had that she was willing to share, she paused.

She knew upon hearing such sad news that Lucas would want to pray. They all bowed their heads while he uttered a short prayer for the dead man and his family and for those affected by his death. He ended with words of gratitude for the safe journey he and his wife had enjoyed and for the good news about his mother-in-law.

"Amen," he said, nodding as he did so. He seemed pleased with the blessings bestowed on them.

"Well," Rose said, breaking the silence after the

prayer. She glanced up at Lucas and Rhonda, their faces aglow with goodness.

Rose remembered how surprised she'd been when she first met them, how she'd thought that to see them with their tattoos and motorcycle regalia, no one would believe Lucas and Rhonda were devoted people of faith.

Their faith wasn't false. It wasn't something they tried to use as a means to say they were better than anyone else. Their commitment was based on the fact that they knew all about hitting rock bottom and they recognized they would have never found their way up had they not had a little help from a higher power. It was as simple to them both as taking twelve steps to sobriety.

Once they got out of prison and made a life for themselves, Lucas and Rhonda didn't become like a lot of folks who hid behind the walls of a church, claiming that they deserved to be there and that they therefore had the right to keep others out.

Rose saw something different in this couple than she remembered seeing in the people she knew from the church pews of her hometown. The Boyds never forgot where it was they'd come from and they never looked at anybody else with the thought that they shouldn't be welcomed or couldn't be saved.

Rose said her own quiet prayer, enjoying a moment of clarity, and then continued what she had been about to say to her friends.

"So, I'm tired and I'm going to go to my trailer and

fix me some dinner. It's been a jam-packed day for me," she said, reaching for the door.

She turned to Lucas and Rhonda. "I'm sorry that you had to leave your work. I know how important that is for you."

"Little sister," Lucas said as he jumped up from his seat at the table and held open the door, "you are also very important to this family. Rhonda and I were speaking of it just last evening. Like our dear Mary, you are a gift from God to Shady Grove." He smiled and his big round face shone.

"He's right, Rose," Rhonda added from her seat at the table. "We thank you for taking care of Mama and for just being here."

"Well, I'm glad you feel that way, since I'm starting to think maybe I brought you bad luck when I came." She turned and looked out to the area where the murder victim had been found. "Two dead men in less than a year," she added somberly.

"Sister Rose, did you ever think that maybe God sent you here for us to be better equipped to handle the deaths of those two dead men?" Lucas asked. "Maybe you're the egg before the chickens," he added with a wink.

"Dead chickens," Rose replied. "But thank you, that's a lovely sentiment just the same. And no, I hadn't thought of that."

Lucas touched her on the shoulder.

"Good night, Rose," Rhonda called out. "Get some rest."

"See you in the morning," Mary added.

"Good night," the nurse replied as she walked out of the office and headed toward her home.

ELEVEN

Rose decided to walk up the path, turning to head along the river before returning to her camper. She wanted to sort through the events of the day, try to think about what she needed to do next.

The bracelet bumped against her leg and she realized that she would not be able to get to bed early like she wanted. Instead, if she followed Ms. Lou Ellen's advice, she would have to wait a couple of hours until everyone was asleep in their campers. She would then have to walk around to the far side of the campground and drop the jewelry somewhere near the trailer now marked with bright yellow caution tape, keeping people away from the site.

She stared down at her watch to see the time and wondered who would be the one to discover the bracelet and whether or not it would fall into the right hands, the hands of the dead man's family.

She thought of a greedy deputy or a curious fisherman and how the bracelet could be lost forever if found by the wrong person. And with that thought, she considered not returning the jewelry to where she had found it, but, rather, waiting until she knew the name of the next of kin and then just sending it straight to them. She moved along the shadows of the descending darkness, unsure of exactly what to do. She stopped at the edge of the water, near one of the small crepe myrtle trees, and sat down.

She reached inside and pulled the now-familiar piece of jewelry out of her pocket. She held it in her hands and then glanced around to see that no one was nearby. When she was sure that she was alone, she clasped the thick cuff-style bracelet around her right wrist. She carefully squeezed the two ends and held up her arm to see how it looked.

In the dimming light of the day, she could make out only the edges of the jewelry. She could not see any of the symbols or even the large turquoise stone. She reached out with her left hand and held the bracelet and her arm against her chest. The dead man's belonging, she thought, somehow connected her to him, and she leaned her head back so that she completely rested against the trunk.

Rose listened to the waves rolling against the shore and considered a family living somewhere hundreds of miles away that could, just at that moment, be finding out about the death of their loved one. Since hearing the recent phone call between Mary and the FBI agent, she knew that the dead man's identity was known and that at some time during the day or during that evening, someone was breaking the news.

She thought about how the next of kin would be given the details. She considered a family preparing to gather around a dinner table, expecting to enjoy a meal together, and receiving a knock on the door or the ring of the phone, which would suddenly change everything about the night, their weeks to come, probably even their lives.

She thought of a grandchild's grief, the littlest one wanting to understand what had happened to the oldest member of the family, the questions about death that a young person so innocently asks. She considered a wife, though she had seen no wedding band on the dead man. Rose thought of how devastating the news would be of a spouse murdered so far away from home. She thought about a son, his anger at some mysterious killer who had so violently stolen away his father.

And then Rose thought of the reaction of a daughter to the news that her father had died. She thought of the sadness, the loss. And then immediately she remembered her own father and the news that she herself had only just received. She recalled how it was, not more than a couple of hours before, to hear a grave report about a family member.

Her father's condition had worsened and at least one person, a person who had lived many years with her as she struggled with her aging parent, a person whom she felt anger toward but whose opinion also mattered to her, had reported that she needed to go home.

Rose held the bracelet closer against her chest and peered out to Memphis, the lights shining across the river. Once she crossed the bridge from Arkansas into

Tennessee, she realized, she would be only one state away from seeing her father. She would be only one state away from the man she had decided almost a year earlier she would never see again.

Now she was being asked to reconsider the choice she had made. She sat at the shore of the river she had come to love and wasn't sure what she was going to do, whether to return to Rocky Mount and her father or not.

It was true, she knew, that she had made her peace with the man who had treated her with such abuse and contempt. She had made peace with the ghosts of her past. Mostly because of her ex-husband's kindness and support throughout the years, she had, by the age of thirty, let go of her long-held bitterness at her father. She drove away from Rocky Mount thinking that she had forgiven him. She had also driven away allowing herself the opportunity not to feel responsible for him any longer.

She had been the one to admit him to the nursing home when his condition had worsened. Later, after making all the arrangements, seeing that he received acceptable care, and helping him settle into his new environment, she had felt released from having to be his caregiver, maybe even his daughter.

And now, right out of the clear blue, just like Ms. Lou Ellen's three-legged dog, her ex-husband had shown up at Shady Grove. Rip had appeared from nowhere and tried to convince her that she was still his caregiver or, at the very least, a daughter who needed to see him. He had tried to say that she had one more responsibility to the man she no longer worried about or fought against.

Rose sat forward, resting her head against her knees, and knew that she wanted to be angry with her ex-husband. She also knew that she had plenty of causes. Aside from his early indiscretions, his affair, now, just after she was starting to heal, starting to make a life for herself, he had come crashing into her new world in his shiny gold Cadillac with his perfect new wife.

He'd rolled into Shady Grove without any fore-warning, without any time for Rose to prepare herself, and then he'd just broken the news that her father was sick and that she needed to let him make peace before he died, as if she owed it to both of them.

Rose thought about Rip with Victoria at his side, the way the younger woman kissed him on the cheek, the easy way her thick hair danced in the breeze, her deep summer tan, even though it was well before tanning season, her long legs, her narrow waist.

Rose felt the knot tighten inside her chest as she remembered the likes and the looks of Victoria Griffith and the fact that Rip had decided to make it part of his business and part of his honeymoon to stop by the campground in West Memphis and counsel his ex-wife about his ex-father-in-law.

"He had no right," she said aloud to herself, and began to see the act as completely selfish on Rip's part. She began thinking about the nerve he'd had in coming and his complete disregard for where she had arrived in her journey in her relationship with her father.

She thought he was arrogant and inappropriate for searching for her and then just dropping by to see her. She thought all of these things, feeling both vindicated and indignant, when suddenly from her perch of righteous anger, she recalled a night with her husband several years before the divorce, the night her father was admitted to the nursing home.

Captain Burns was to be released from the hospital after becoming gravely ill due to the damaged condition of his liver. He had spent more than three weeks in the intensive care unit, two more weeks that followed on a medical-surgical unit. Rose, working as a nurse in the same facility, spent a great deal of time checking on him and talking to the doctors about his prognosis, his living situation, and the best-possible scenario for him as a single person with liver disease and someone beginning to demonstrate signs of dementia or even, perhaps, Alzheimer's.

Before his hospitalization, no one was completely sure about his mental condition. He was forgetful and there was a history of him wandering into unfamiliar places. There were also a few reports from neighbors of him acting in a disorienting or confused manner. He had even wrecked his car and started a small kitchen fire, but these were only occasional incidents.

When confronted, he seemed clear, and he certainly

refused to accept that anything was wrong with him. He absolutely dismissed any notion that he was functioning at a diminished capacity. There was never a discussion with him about making any living changes.

After the hospital stay of so many weeks, however, with his physical weakness and his observed mental deficiencies, all of the medical personnel working with Captain Burns agreed that upon release from the hospital he would not be able to live alone.

Rose had spent days, weeks even, in conversations with social workers, doctors, friends, her husband, and her brother. She had tried, albeit unsuccessfully, to talk with her father. Finally, after much deliberation and a decision that she would not let him live with her, she found a place where she believed he would receive the best care. With much agonizing and trepidation, she signed the papers committing her father to a nursing home.

It had been an extremely difficult time for her. Without her brother's input or assistance, she was forced to make the decision by herself, and when her father discovered that it was she who had committed him, he was enraged.

He was so upset with her, in fact, that the day he was to be transferred to the long-term-care facility, he had to be placed in restraints. He had made it very clear not only that he was not going to go to the nursing home without a fight and would escape if taken there but that he was also going to kill the person who had signed the papers admitting him.

When her father, heavily sedated, was taken by ambulance to his new home, it was strongly suggested to his daughter that she not visit for a few days. The director of the facility had called her personally and said that it would be most helpful to have a little while to allow the new patient, her father, to become acquainted with his surroundings, that they have some time to find more effective means to support Captain Burns with this difficult transition, and that it would just simply be best for her to wait a couple of weeks before making her first visit.

Receiving such advice brought lots of emotion to the surface for Rose. In spite of the troubled relationship she had endured, she was still her father's only caregiver and she remained concerned about the man she had hated for so many years. She was, however, also relieved not to have to deal with him in this new setting, relieved to have some time to rest after the long and exhausting period she had endured while his mental condition and physical illness had worsened and since he had been hospitalized. She was facing so many complicated emotions that she didn't know how to feel about anything.

The day her father had been admitted to the nursing home, Rose returned to her house from work, worn thin from worry and fatigue, to find that Rip had been home all day and had prepared the only meal she had ever known him to fix.

This night, this dinner—this was the memory she

thought of as the day of her ex-husband's sudden visitation, the day of the discovery of a murdered man, drifted into the darkness there by the Mississippi River.

On the night of her father's admissions, Rip met Rose at the door with a glass of wine and one long-stem red rose. He then led her straight to the table, guiding her into her seat. He fed her baked chicken, which she remembered was kept in the oven much too long, mashed potatoes that were so dry and lumpy that she had choked on her first spoonful, and a salad made with too much dressing. The dessert, she recalled with a smile, had been perfect, however. He had bought two pieces of cake from a local bakery and had added a big helping of ice cream on the side.

He didn't say much about the day, about what he understood his wife had been wrestling with. However, after explaining his methods of cooking, about everything he had learned and done, how he'd actually enjoyed being in the kitchen, he did finally say something about the decision his wife had made.

Rose still remembered how his simple way of summing things up, his firm gesture of empathy, had melted away so much of her sorrow. "Rose, you've done the right thing," he said as she finished the dessert. "Your father needs the care of somebody else, somebody who doesn't have all the history that you have."

She'd swallowed and listened.

"Those nurses there will be able to make him take his medicine, eat his meals, and they won't allow him to hurt anybody. You can't do that. He has had power over you your whole life and he knows that; as long as he knows that, you can't take care of him. You just can't. And it's really okay that somebody else does."

She recalled how the words felt that night so long ago, the kindness in them, the generosity and wisdom behind them. On that complicated and difficult night, she loved her husband for knowing the right thing to say at a time when she felt so empty of pardon for herself. And as Rose rested against a river tree at the end of the day he had come to her new home on the arm of a new wife, she knew that in spite of everything else Rip had done to her, done to the marriage, because of that one pure evening, she could not hate him or demonize him.

With a plate of dry chicken and lumpy potatoes, with a slice of chocolate cake and the words she was desperate to hear, he had freed her from the bondage of old chains. He had given her permission to unbind herself from her father's heavy hand. Although there were lots of reasons to despise him, Rose knew, because of that night, she could not dismiss the man who had only months later chosen someone else to love.

She sat for just a few minutes longer down by the riverside, thinking of love and loss, of choices and betrayals. She realized that she had only one thing that had to be done before this night was over, that she didn't have to make any decision right then about her own family.

She took off the bracelet and slipped it in her jacket pocket.

She did not have to decide about returning to Rocky Mount or whether to give her father room to say what he might or might not desire to say. She did not have to leave Shady Grove anytime soon.

Now, she told herself, she would only need to return what wasn't hers. After that, she would be out of the business of another family's crisis and she would then figure out how to handle her own.

TWELVE

It was almost midnight when Rose got up from the bed after watching a few shows on television and flipping through some magazines, trying not to nod off. She figured it would be easier to stay awake until it was time to go, rather than set the alarm and get only a couple of hours of sleep.

She already had on her thick blue sweatpants, her black hooded sweatshirt, and her dark cap. When she decided it was the right time to return the bracelet, all she needed to add to her wardrobe were her shoes, which she slipped on at the door. Once she was completely dressed, she quietly left her camper. Adorned in such dark and heavy clothes, she was prepared both for the chill in the night air and for hiding in the darkness.

She crept along the driveway, past the other campers, hearing only the noises of the river at night. A barn owl called from across the shore, searching for his evening meal. Crickets sang from the tall grass lining the pond and from the long, empty fields. The slow waves fell against the banks. It was mostly quiet, and Rose was soon distracted from her task as she stopped to listen to the sounds she had grown to love.

A recent resident of Shady Grove, Rose often went outside for late-night walks. She and Tom would meet on the path between the campground and the small lot where he lived. They would walk through the memorial site where his friend Lawrence Franklin was buried and where the ghosts of fallen slaves had finally settled and rested.

When they met that way, late at night, they spoke very little as they moved along the trails, and during those long dark hikes along the shore and across dusty paths, Rose had fallen in love with the life that emerged on the banks of the Mississippi River in West Memphis.

She shook the gentle thoughts from her head and resumed her walk, moving beyond the campsites and into the area that had been closed to campers. She hurried ahead and continued to think about Tom and the way he had softened her spirit, opened her knotted heart. She missed him and wondered what he would say about this late-night adventure, her theft of the bracelet, and then her return at midnight to the crime scene.

She hoped that he would be home the next day so that she could include him in all of her deliberations and decision making. She knew that had he been with her during the day, he probably would have told her that she shouldn't always follow Ms. Lou Ellen's advice. He had mentioned to her before that although he was deeply committed to their mutual friend, he had discovered that the older woman was not always the right one to seek out for counsel.

"Lou Ellen has some unique ideas," he had said when Rose was thinking about answering a chain letter that Ms. Lou Ellen had copied and sent, a chain letter promising money and good health. "She's smart, but she's not always careful," he told Rose. "And she somehow always manages to escape her ill-planned schemes, but she's lucky that way. I'm not sure everybody else has that much good fortune."

Surely, Rose thought, he knows her better than I. And as she moved toward the part of the campground where she had found the dead man, the part that had been recently sealed off and had, by that late hour, developed an eerie air about it, she considered that maybe this hadn't been the best advice to heed. She decided to complete the task as quickly as she could and return home.

She headed toward the small field, hurrying over to where she had first found the bracelet. She walked across the overgrown path and through the patch of weeds. She planned to go just a few more steps, drop the dead man's jewelry in the grass, and then swiftly head back to her camper, forgetting about the interesting symbols, the beautiful turquoise, and the motive for murder. She was going to let the sheriff tend to the homicide and she was going to spend her time trying to figure out what to do about her own situation.

Rose was only a few yards from the old Coachmen when she pulled the bracelet from the front pocket of her sweatshirt, held it tightly in her hand, used her shirt to wipe off her prints, and knelt down to dispose herself of it. Just in that instant, she saw a light shine right above her head, right where, only seconds before, she had been standing. She remained in a squatting position and carefully spun around, replacing the bracelet back into her pocket.

The light was coming from a boat docking not more than fifty yards away from where Rose was kneeling. She heard the voices of at least two men as they gathered very near to her. One of them seemed to be giving instructions as the vessel pulled up on the bank; another one was shining the light in her direction, reporting any activity around the camper and also explaining where they were on the river. She wasn't sure if there was anyone else with them or not.

She froze, uncertain if she had been noticed. Since she thought the light had shone above her head and because it didn't seem that the men were in a hurry to get to where she was, she hoped that she had not been discovered.

Slowly, she crawled through the grass, under the yellow police tape, and over to the scene of the crime. She heard the men coming toward her. The beam of the flashlight moved all around her as she crouched down. Without knowing what else to do, she felt for the steps of the trailer, gently crept to the bottom one, reached up, and was able to grab the handle to the closed door.

With the light dancing along the side of the trailer, Rose could tell that the window she had broken earlier in the day had been sealed with duct tape. But in turning the handle, she immediately knew that the door had been left unlocked. Hardly believing her good fortune, she remembered Tom's thoughts about Ms. Lou Ellen, and she silently thanked the heavens for lending her some of her friend's excellent luck.

She opened the narrow door and quickly moved up the steps and slid in. She felt her pulse race, and small beads of sweat formed on the top of her lip and along her brow line.

She was uncertain if the men had seen her movement. She sat with her back against the closed door and glanced around for anything in the trailer that she might use as a weapon. She also looked for a place to hide.

Though she knew it was hardly a means of real protection, she reached up and turned the lock on the handle. Just as she spun the lock, she heard the voices. The men were just outside the trailer.

"Shh," one of the voices said.

Rose sat completely still.

"What was that?" the man asked.

There was another pause.

Rose tried to think if she recognized either of the voices, but she didn't. She felt the weight on the steps just behind her. She closed her eyes, preparing for the worst.

"Probably just mice or something," replied the other man.

Someone fiddled with the handle. Rose held her breath.

"It's locked," the voice at the door said.

"Well, the window is broke. Just cut the tape." The other voice sounded as if the man had now moved over to an area in front of the camper, near the truck.

Rose heard a rustling. She could feel the trailer shake as the man tried to break open the taped area around the shattered window. He pulled a bit, said a few curse words as he tore at the tape, and then Rose felt him move away. He was walking around to the front to join the other man.

When she knew he was away from the door, Rose remembered that there was a small storage area beneath the bed in the rear of the camper. She crawled toward it, moving through the mounds of strewn supplies and belongings that were still on the floor. She assumed the body had been taken out and delivered to the morgue.

She felt under the bed for the small door to the storage area, found it, and opened it. Although she figured that she was probably too large to fit, she drew in a deep breath and forced herself in. Then she quietly pulled the small door shut. She heard the click.

Fortunately, she didn't think the men now standing somewhere near the truck, away from the camper, had heard it. Neither one of them seemed to be returning to the door.

Rose waited. She couldn't make out the conversation they were having, although she did hear the two men discussing something. She heard only a muffled string of words. She felt a knock near where she lay and then heard a clamor, like metal on metal, somewhere near the hitch.

Minutes passed and Rose heard and felt nothing. She was thinking that the men had left and that she was going to be able to crawl out of the dead man's camper and finally get to her own.

She thought that maybe her good fortune, her friend's good fortune, was even more substantial than Tom believed. She told herself that she would have to remember to inform him about this and see if she could get a copy of the chain letter that she had, based upon his advice, torn up and thrown away.

She waited a bit longer. She didn't want to be too impatient. After all, the men hadn't just come to the trailer to sightsee, she realized. They were there for something. She knew that their plans, whatever they were, would not be scrapped by a few inches of duct tape.

She wondered if they were there for the bracelet, which she felt in her front pocket, just beneath her ribs. Because of their arrival, she had not had the chance to discard it. She wondered if they were the killers, if they would kill her, too, if they found her.

With that thought, she felt her pulse pick up speed and she tried to think of something else, like how she was sure she would get out of this predicament soon and how the two or three men who had boated up the river to Shady Grove had found what they were searching for in the dead man's truck and were probably gone for good now. She tried to continue focusing on that possibility.

It remained silent. Rose heard nothing, felt nothing. She waited a few minutes more. She wanted to be completely sure that the coast was clear, that the men had departed.

She was just about to open the compartment, get out, and make a run for it, when suddenly she felt the trailer shift and then lunge forward. Much to her surprise, it stopped and then started again.

The trailer was moving. The men were stealing the rig. And apparently, from all of the bumps she was feeling, they were heading out of Shady Grove by a way other than the main driveway. And then just as she realized what was happening, Rose was thrown against the rear wall of the tiny storage area under the bed. With the weight and sudden impact of her body, the wall collapsed; and Rose found herself in a modified section that had been cleverly concealed.

Her neck and back ached a little from the fall and she felt something long and awkward beneath her. The trailer picked up speed, but because she was now in such a small area, she rolled only a little from side to side.

Rose had not noticed this compartment when she had been in the trailer earlier. She knew this storage bin was in the camper when she had looked under the bed after she had discovered the dead man. And as she lay in the small area as the camper was being pulled along the road, she remembered that with the storage door open and the contents emptied and thrown about the camper, she had seen only the rear wall. This, she realized as she lay there, was something added to the Coachmen, something she had not expected. She had crashed into a secret compartment.

Once the road seemed to smooth out and the jerking movement eased, Rose reached up and felt around her. It was dark where she was and all that she could sense was the short, thin partition on the side from which she had fallen and a long wall that was the exterior of the camper on the other. Above her head was just the top of the storage compartment, which would have been the bottom of the bed.

She felt the camper take a quick turn to the right, and when she reached beneath her, bracing herself, she felt thick pieces of wood, two long ones on both sides studded with smooth round stones, and small, narrow pieces that were attached.

She grabbed the longer, thicker rails beneath her and held on, discovering that the structure was so perfectly positioned that even with the sharp turns and the bumpy ride, Rose was able to keep from being tossed about.

THIRTEEN

Rose lay quietly as she heard things slide and careen outside the storage compartment. All of the dead man's belongings that she had seen earlier scattered along the floor and across the camper were now being thrown around. She realized that she was safe from being hit by the pots and pans, the shoes and books, because of where she was hiding. She congratulated herself for being so resourceful.

She had closed the door to the storage compartment under the bed when she'd squeezed in; and since the small area where she lay was located far enough away from the door, she knew that even if it came open, she was protected from being hammered by the unsecured objects. Rose was grateful for that.

She was also grateful that she did not have a problem with claustrophobia. The tiny spot where she had landed barely had room for her to lay with her arms by her sides. She felt like she was in the trunk of a car or a narrow box. And with those two images suddenly introduced into her thoughts, she turned her head so that she could face the door to the storage compartment at the other end from where she lay. She wanted to remind herself that she did, in fact, still have a way out even if it took her right into the path of the killers and thieves.

As the road seemed to flatten and straighten out, the truck and trailer moving more smoothly, Rose assumed that they had made their way to the interstate and the items inside the camper had settled. Once this happened, Rose began to understand the gravity of her situation. She realized that she was being taken somewhere and that eventually the camper would be searched and she would be discovered. She lay noiselessly and wondered what on earth she would do now that she was stuck inside a stolen vehicle.

She thought that if the trailer continued to travel at such a smooth pace, she could crawl out of the storage area, make her way to the front door, and jump out. She guessed that since there was only a hitch between the truck and the trailer, the men would not register extra movement from where she was.

She considered the difficulty of such an event and then also the risks, such as the likely damage she would do to herself when she leaped, how she could easily land beneath the wheels of the trailer or underneath another vehicle that could be following behind, and immediately began to have second thoughts.

She thought of the very real possibility that the

driver and his cohort would see her when she jumped, quickly pull off the road, and find her once she landed.

Upon estimating the risks and probable consequences of that action, she decided to think of another idea. She figured that since she had not noticed this rear compartment before that maybe if she was able to secure the fake wall back in place, the thieves wouldn't notice it, either, when they entered the camper, at least not right away, thus allowing her some time to sneak out later when they weren't around.

She felt around her body, searching with her fingers for the broken wall and discovered that idea wasn't going to work, either. The thin partition that she had crashed through was now in pieces beneath and beside her. Without glue or a hammer and nails, she would certainly not be able to put it back together. She told herself that she would have to think of something else.

Rose did not know what to do. She tried imagining lots of other escapes, but nothing seemed logical or doable. As she lay in the confined area and tried to calculate her next move, fighting to stay alert, she found that the noise of the highway beneath her, the late hour, and the exhaustion of her adventure had begun to make her sleepy.

Rose was uncomfortable in her hiding place, and at first she decided this was probably a good thing. The objects poking in her spine and neck would keep her awake, and she knew she had a much better chance of staying alive if she stayed awake. The longer she rode, however, the more painful her position became.

Finally, when she could not stand it any longer and her body started to ache, Rose reached beneath her, straightening the broken pieces of wood, trying to cover the things that were jabbing into her spine. She again felt the short, knobby sticks, how they were evenly spaced, how they seemed to fit into the long vertical limbs, and she realized what it was she lay upon. It was a ladder, a long, narrow wooden ladder.

Rose couldn't understand why the owner of the camper had gone to such lengths to square away a simple ladder; but she was pleased that she was able to solve at least one of her riddles. She continued to pull and reposition the broken pieces of wood from the wall to cover the areas between the ladder rungs.

Finally, pulling her arms out from beneath her, she folded them across her chest and stretched out her legs completely. She realized that she had created a flat, level surface for herself.

Once she managed this rearrangement and relaxed, her body in a completely supine position, she discovered that the compartment was quite a cozy hiding place. And though she tried to stay awake, keep her eyes open, and plan her escape, in her newly achieved comfort and in her state of fatigue, Rose nodded off.

She was anxious and panicked about her circumstances, but Rose was also tired. She could not keep herself from falling asleep and she could not stop the dream.

Rose leaned down and away into the far-reaching well of somebody else's memory. She fell, like Alice in her wonderland, deep and long into the vision of another's restless soul. She tumbled against walls studded with old diamonds, gemstones, frozen tears of a snatched and disappeared people. She heard only small cries, those of children, old women; the sound was faint and broken and yet never completely covered up or lost.

Rose dreamed of the brightest colors, the blue of the morning sky, the red of the summer sun, of the narrow cup of roses, of blood. She slid and dropped and flew through wisps of a fragrant smoke, sage grass and cedar, through clouds of violent thunder pealing like the distant beating of a drum.

She spiraled down and down, deep into cold, dark layers of earth, and though she reached out for a means to catch herself, a rock to hold, a limb or rope, there was nothing but the wall of tears and never a place to land.

She was falling into endless space, past the colors, past the sun, until there was only darkness, only the faint cries, the rhythmic pulse of a drum, and the cold, thick darkness, with no way up to the light.

When she woke, she was immediately reminded of her dire circumstances and she was also unsettled by the dream. It was so unfamiliar to her, so foreign, she was convinced it belonged to someone else. She pulled herself out of the dream and discovered that she had no idea where she was or what time it was. She did not know how long she had been asleep. She made herself focus and realized that all she knew was that the vehicle had ceased traveling and that she was once again in danger of being discovered.

Rose waited. She was still on her back, jammed in the confined area, her body now stiff from the amount of time she had been in that one position. Unsure of the hour, she wished she had been wearing her watch.

She waited a bit longer. She heard nothing, felt nothing. There was no movement outside the front of the camper near the hitch, no sounds anywhere around her. Finally, she decided she had tarried as long as she could. She raised herself up, knocking her head on the top of the compartment that was under the bed. The trailer rocked. She quickly lay back down.

After hearing no one enter, she raised herself up again, this time more carefully, and rolled out of the hidden bin. She slid slowly to the door of the storage area, then waited. Still there was nothing. She slowly pushed at the door until it opened slightly.

It was dark, though Rose could see a bright light shining through the window next to the overturned table in the center of the camper. She stayed in her supine position behind the barely opened door for a few minutes, trying to get her bearings. When she still heard and saw nothing, she pushed the door and crawled out. She quietly closed the door and moved over to the large window, where she knelt and peeked out.

Once she had adjusted her eyes to the electric lights outside, she could make out the interstate in the distance, only a few cars and trucks snaking along the highway. She could see the signs of gas stations and a few fast-food restaurants.

She thought at first that perhaps they had pulled into a truck stop, that maybe the two men had gotten hungry or needed to relieve themselves—something she was realizing she was needing to do—but as she glanced around through the tiny openings through the curtains, she realized that they were parked in the rear of a motel. From the other window, the one by the kitchen sink, she could see the long, straight row of rooms—most of them darkened, shades drawn, with no movement from within.

Rose grew excited about the possibility of an easy escape. Apparently, she surmised, the men had stopped to get a room and she was going to be able to get out of the camper without being noticed.

She crept toward the door of the trailer and was just about to push it open when she heard a vehicle driving up. She dropped down and crawled toward the rear of the camper, pushing through the fallen and broken debris. She rolled into the storage compartment again, pulling the door closed behind her.

It was a truck, a big one; she could tell by the sounds of the engine and then the brakes. She heard a door open, a few grunts as the driver seemed to get down from the seat, and then the door close. She heard footsteps that seemed to be moving away and then nothing. It grew silent again.

Rose waited a few minutes and then slowly cracked open the door. When she did, the light hit something that shined on the wall beside her. She reached over and saw that it was two keys on a small silver ring, hanging on a nail. She grabbed them, not sure what they fit, and then crawled to the camper door.

She unlocked the handle, opened the door, and peeked out. She saw no one, just the recently arrived eighteen-wheel truck parked close beside the trailer.

She stood up on the top step, stretched her back and hips, remembered the keys in her hand, climbed down the steps, walked over to the truck with the New Mexico plates, the truck that belonged to the dead man, and, just because she was feeling incredibly lucky, stuck one of the keys in the door.

It didn't fit. She glanced around again nervously. She tried the other key, and much to her surprise, the door unlocked. Rose opened it, jumped inside, and slid down in the seat. Carefully, she reached up and put the other key into the ignition. It was a perfect fit. She sat up, glancing in all directions, and still saw no one. Without having any idea where she was or how she would get back to West Memphis, Rose started the truck, and gradually, easily, pulled out of the parking lot.

She came to the driveway of the motel, looked left and then right, then pressed her foot hard against the gas pedal. Gunning the motor, Rose drove the stolen vehicles toward what she hoped was an interstate.

FOURTEEN

Who is this?" The gruff voice called out into the receiver after Rose had dialed the sheriff's home number and awakened him from a deep sleep.

"Collect call from Rose Franklin," the recording from the phone company reported.

"Rose Franklin?" he asked, surprise in the tone of his voice.

There was a pause.

The recording started to repeat itself.

"Yes, yes," he replied.

Rose was put through.

"Rose?" he asked, sounding very disoriented. "What time is it?"

"About six-fifteen," she said, "in the morning." She had found out the time from a radio station in the truck.

"You got some good reason for calling me this early in the day?" he asked. He rubbed his eyes and sat up a little in the bed. "Collect, I might add."

"I . . . I think so," she stammered, unsure of how to explain her situation. There was another pause.

"Well, I'm waiting." He had put on his glasses and sat up in his bed.

"Where are you?" he asked.

"Checotah," she replied.

"Oklahoma?" he responded.

"Yes, that's right."

"You want to tell me why you're in Checotah, Oklahoma, and why you decided to call me?" he asked.

Rose could tell that Sheriff Montgomery was not a morning person.

"I was kidnapped," she said, thinking that a little drama might ease the rest of the story she was going to have to tell. She was hoping for some sympathy.

"Kidnapped?" he asked, not sounding quite as sympathetic as she'd been expecting. "From where?"

"Shady Grove," she told him. She waited.

"How come nobody else reported this?" he asked.

She hadn't thought of that.

"It just happened," she replied. "Last night." She hesitated. "Well, more like this morning, about midnight." Would that be last night or this morning? she wondered. "I haven't been missed yet," she said, thinking that sounded very believable. "Nobody knows I'm gone."

"From your place?" he asked, now interested.

"What? Uh, well, no, not really," she said.

"From the office?"

"Uh, well, no not there, either." She wasn't sure the drama idea was turning out to be such a good one.

"Rose, are you all right?" he asked, sounding very fatherly.

She liked that.

"Yes," she said. "I'm pretty sure I lost them."

"The kidnappers?"

"Right."

"And you're in Oklahoma?"

"Checotah," she said again. "Is that the name of an Indian tribe?"

He wasn't going to answer her question. "Rose, have you called the police there?"

"No, I called you first."

"Then hang up and dial nine one one," he replied. "Tell them what's happened. Then call me back."

"Well, I kinda think you might want to hear the story first," she said timidly.

"Okay."

Rose hesitated.

"I'm listening." He was sounding perturbed again.

"Okay, last night I went over to the camper," she began.

"Your camper?" he asked.

"No, the dead man's camper."

"After I told you to quit snooping around," he said.

She waited. She didn't have a good response.

"Yeah, well, I needed to see about something," she replied, trying to figure out a way she could get around having to tell him about the bracelet.

"And what time was this that you had to go out to a sealed crime scene and see about something?"

"About midnight."

There was no reply.

"I'm still listening," he said.

"So, while I'm there, I hear two or three men coming toward the camper,"

"The dead man's camper, the one sealed off with police tape that says 'Do not enter.'"

She could tell he was angry with her.

"That would be right," she replied.

"Go on," he instructed.

"So, I hear them coming in my direction and I jumped in the camper and locked the door." She felt her voice grow in excitement. It was a good story, she thought.

"They tried to get in, but the window was duct-taped. I guess Deputy Roy did that." She waited, but the sheriff did not reply.

"So then I hid in the storage compartment under the bed and waited for them to come in, but they never did."

There was still no answer.

"But they drove off with the camper, with me in it."

"In the storage compartment," he finally said.

"Right," she said, deciding not to add the part about the secret area she had fallen into. She didn't want to overload him with too much information. Then she remembered the dream, or parts of the dream, but she decided not to share that, either.

"And they drove you to Checotah, Oklahoma, and let you out."

"No," she said loudly, thinking he didn't appreciate the danger she had just faced, the courage she had displayed, the brilliant escape she had created for herself.

"They drove to Henryetta, Oklahoma, parked at a motel, and got out. When they were gone, I jumped out of the camper, found an extra set of truck keys, and drove down the interstate for about an hour and then stopped in Checotah to call you." She took a breath and continued. "I think that if we call the police in Henryetta, they could probably catch the men. It hasn't been that long since I drove off. They're more than likely still asleep in the motel room."

Sheriff Montgomery sighed. At least Rose thought it sounded like a sigh. She wasn't sure.

"Can you identify these two men?" he asked.

She hadn't thought of that. "No," she replied. "I only heard them talk."

"So, you think I should call the Oklahoma police."

"In Henryetta," she said.

"I should call the Henryetta, Oklahoma, police and tell them to go to the—Do you know the name of the motel?" he asked.

She hadn't thought of that, either. She had been in such a hurry getting out of the parking lot, she had forgotten to notice the name of the place where they had parked.

"It . . . it was the something motel," she said.

"Okay," he replied, trying to get her to see how ridiculous her story was now becoming. "I call the Henryetta police and tell them to find 'the something motel' and search for two men who checked in late last night."

"More like this morning," she said, thinking it was actually a fine story. "That can't be too hard; it had to have been really late."

"Two men who checked in this morning," he continued, "who can't be identified."

"Oh," she said. "I guess that might take some time." She was beginning to see the difficulty in her plan.

"Yeah, I think we need a little more information before we go knocking on the doors of every room of every motel in Henryetta, Oklahoma, searching for two men who stole a camper but then stopped along the way to sleep."

Rose then understood that Sheriff Montgomery didn't believe the story she had given him. "You think I'm making this up?" she asked incredulously.

The sheriff blew out a long breath. "No," he said. "I think you've been messing around with something I told you not to and now you've gotten yourself mixed up with some people who could be very dangerous."

She didn't respond.

"Where are you exactly in Checotah, Oklahoma?"

"A rest stop, off of I-Forty," she told him, starting to feel a little weepy.

"Just wait there," he instructed. "I'll call somebody to come for you." He hesitated, expecting her to respond. "Okay?" he asked, trying to sound a little more understanding.

There was still no reply.

"Rose, okay?" he asked again.

She mumbled, "Okay."

"Do you remember the exit number?"

"No."

"It's a highway rest stop in Checotah?"

"Yes."

"And you're in an old Ford pickup pulling a tan motor home, both with New Mexico plates?" he asked, not sure his memory was correct.

"Gray," she said.

"What?"

"The camper," she said, "it's a gray Coachmen."

"Okay," he said, now in a softer tone. "I'll call Highway Patrol. It may take a little while," he added. "You going to be all right?"

"Yes, I'm fine," she told him, hoping that he wouldn't recognize the vulnerability in her voice.

"Okay, go to the truck and lock the doors."

She was about to hang up the phone.

"And Rose," the sheriff added, "call me back if you need me."

"Thank you," she said.

She placed the receiver in the cradle, and after glancing in all directions and seeing no one around, she quickly left the phone booth.

FIFTEEN

Rose went inside the rest area to use the bathroom. She saw only one other car parked in the lot, and she watched a man walking to it as she was entering the facility. He got in the car and drove away. He hadn't seemed to notice her, and there appeared to be no one else around.

She headed inside the ladies' room, then, after exiting the stall, moved slowly over to the sink and splashed cold water on her face. She studied herself in the mirror and wiped her face with a paper napkin. She knew that she was lucky to have gotten away from the men who stole the camper, but she wondered how much trouble she would be in once she returned to West Memphis.

She pulled on the sides of her face, giving herself a lift, thinking she had grown old in the last forty-eight hours. Using her fingers, she tried to straighten her hair, fix herself up a little before facing the firing squad of police officers that Sheriff Montgomery was sure to send her way. She knew that she was in for another long day.

When she walked out, she was surprised to see that there was a uniformed officer standing beside the truck. He was peeking inside the cab when she walked up, looking in through the driver's window.

She glanced around for the police car; but she saw

only a dark SUV parked behind the camper. Remembering that the Highway Patrol often drove unmarked vehicles, she thought nothing of it.

"Rose Franklin?" the man asked when he saw her coming near.

She felt him watching her as she moved closer. He seemed to be sizing her up, trying to figure out the situation.

"You Rose Franklin?" he asked again. His hand was positioned on the top of the weapon that hung from his belt.

He was nice-looking, about thirty or thirty-five, she guessed. He was tall, of medium build, had short brown hair, and was wearing a crisp navy suit with a badge over the left front pocket of his shirt. He carried his hat under his arm.

He had on dark sunglasses, which Rose thought was a bit over the top, since it was so early in the morning. He held a clipboard next to his hat. There were handcuffs hanging off of his belt and the gun, a small pistol in a holster attached to the right side. He was standing straight, at attention, appearing ready for police business.

"Yes," she replied, walking up to him, "I'm Rose Franklin."

"I got the call to come and check on you." He turned away from her and studied the vehicle, his eyes moving from end to end.

"The West Memphis sheriff said you were in some trouble?" He phrased it like a question.

144

"You got here really fast," she said. "Did Sheriff Montgomery call you directly?"

The young officer shook his head. "Got the call on the scanner," he said. "I was on the interstate, just a couple of exits up. Now, what happened exactly?" he asked, acting as if he was not interested in small talk or explaining his whereabouts.

Suddenly, Rose was not sure about wanting to tell the same story she had told to Sheriff Montgomery. She wasn't convinced that she wanted to call what had occurred a kidnapping. She tried to think of another way to explain what she was doing in Checotah.

"I was in a campground in West Memphis," she began. "Shady Grove?"

The man nodded his head as if he had heard of the place. "On the river," he replied.

"Right." She supposed that most folks in that part of the country were familiar with the geography of the Mississippi. She stopped because she thought he might say something more, but he was silent.

"Well, anyway, I was just walking around and I heard some men coming toward me. So I got scared and I ducked in the camper. The next thing I knew, I was being driven off." With this officer, she decided, less was more. She might as well save all the details for the police in West Memphis.

"While you were in it?" he asked, glancing around the parking lot.

Rose followed his eyes. There were still no other

cars around. She nodded when he turned back to face her.

"And when these men stopped in Henryetta at a motel, you climbed out of the camper and drove to Checotah?"

She wondered how he knew about Henryetta, but she figured that the sheriff had mentioned all of that when he called in the report. The officer seemed to know everything she had told Sheriff Montgomery.

She nodded again.

"You get a look at the men?" he asked.

Rose shook her head. She knew her story wasn't going to be very believable. Then she thought about getting back to West Memphis. She wasn't sure whether the police would take her or if somebody would have to come and get her.

She wondered if Tom was still in Fort Smith. She thought that if he were there, it would make the most sense to have him drive up to Checotah and get her. She considered whether or not the officer might let her use his phone to call Tom, then decided that she would ask him later.

"So." The young officer had taken out a pen and appeared to be making a few notes on the paper in his clipboard. "You were in the camper most of the night?" He waited for a response.

Rose nodded.

"Did you notice anything different inside the camper while you hid?" he asked.

Rose thought that was an odd question to ask at the

beginning of his report, but she figured he had his own reasons for how he conducted his investigation.

The officer searched around the lot again. A car pulled in and stopped on the other side of the rest area. He appeared to be watching it with a great amount of interest.

"Did you see anything out of the ordinary while you were in the camper?" he asked again, his tone a bit more agitated. Then he cleared his throat and asked it another way. "Do you have any idea as to why the two men may have wanted to steal the vehicle?"

Rose thought that was a logical line of questioning. She remembered the bracelet and reached down. It was still in her front pocket. She knew that was going to take some explaining, too.

She was about to answer his question by saying that she didn't have any thoughts about why they were stealing the camper, that she had not seen anything unique while she was hiding inside, and then she suddenly thought of the ladder, how odd it was that the dead man had secured it, hidden it so far away. Though she could not understand what would have been so important about a ladder for a camper, she wondered, because of the officer's question, if that was what the men had been searching for.

"I hid in the storage area under the bed," she told the officer as a means of having the story unfold. Then she stopped.

"What's your name?" she asked, realizing he hadn't introduced himself.

"Caldwell," he said. "Go ahead," he instructed, appearing very interested in her answer.

"So, I was hiding in there, thinking that might be the best place. It's very small," she said.

The officer nodded as if he knew that.

"And when the camper made a turn, I fell through the rear of it, into another little holding area, another compartment, modified," she explained. Then she paused again and asked, "Are you Highway Patrol?"

"Right," he replied, sounding a bit put off by her questions. "Officer Caldwell of the Oklahoma Highway Patrol," and he reached to his pocket and held out his badge, which confirmed only his name.

Rose looked it over and nodded. "You work all night?" she asked. She'd stopped telling the story because it had dawned on her that it might just help her case if she was thought to be polite and forth-coming by the first responding officer. She under-stood that she was going to be in trouble when she returned to Arkansas, so she figured she might as well have at least one lawman on her side. Besides, she thought, observing him very closely, he really was quite good-looking.

"All night," he replied affirmatively. "I work the late shift." He did not seem to appreciate her attempt at light conversation.

Rose wondered what color his eyes were and was hoping he would remove his sunglasses.

He quickly returned to the line of questioning,

"When you fell through to this holding area, what did you find?" He was no longer taking notes.

"Just a ladder," she replied.

Immediately, the officer stepped away from Rose and moved to the camper door. He walked up the steps, reached up, and discovered that it was locked. He turned to her. "You have the key?" he asked.

Rose nodded and pointed inside the truck.

"I'd like for you to get that for me," he said, now having stepped down and shifted his body slightly away from the camper.

Rose reached inside the truck and got an extra camper key that she had found in the ashtray. She shut the door and headed in the officer's direction. She opened the door and was going to let him enter first. He started to go up the steps and then seemed to think better of it.

"Why don't you go and get it," he suggested, glimpsing around the parking lot again. "I'll go radio my office to let them know that I've found you and that you're okay."

Rose shrugged; she figured he should do whatever he needed to do. She walked up the steps and into the camper. It's such a mess, she thought as she inched her way across stacks of clothes and strewn objects. She knelt down and opened the storage area, lay down and rolled inside. She was growing tired of the small hiding place. She slid toward the rear of the compartment, where she had fallen and slept and dreamed such an odd dream. She reached around and felt for the ladder.

Without any light, Rose was unsuccessful in knowing how to pull the ladder out from the compartment. It was tied or nailed to the floor and she was unable to unloosen it.

It soon became uncomfortable for Rose lying on her back. She attempted to free the ladder for about ten minutes, working on both ends, trying to pull it out. But she couldn't figure out how to loosen it from the walls of the hidden area.

After a few more minutes, she realized she was not going to be able to release it by herself. She rolled away from the rear area, squeezed out from the storage compartment, stood up inside the camper, and headed for the door.

"I'm going to need some help," she said before she got all the way out of the camper.

Rose stood on the top step. She was surprised to see that the black SUV and Officer Caldwell were gone. She glanced at the entryway of the rest stop and noticed two Highway Patrol cars pulling in, heading in her direction. She turned so she could see the exit and saw only a small cloud of dust as a vehicle sped onto the interstate.

SIXTEEN

Rose Franklin?" the officer from the first car asked as he stepped out from the driver's side.

Rose was still staring in the direction of the exit. She was puzzled by Patrolman Caldwell's quick departure. When she saw the two cars pulling into the rest stop, she simply thought he had called the station and was receiving backup.

"Yes," she said, "I'm Rose Franklin."

She waited for him to introduce himself and explain what he was doing there and why the first officer had departed so quickly.

"I'm Officer Paul Lincoln," he said, and immediately presented her with a business card with his name and information.

Rose studied it. Then she peered up at the man in front of her. She noticed a few differences between Officer Lincoln's uniform and the uniform of the man who had only recently left.

Under Officer Lincoln's badge there was a identification card, clearly showing a photo of the man standing in front of her, as well as his rank. She studied the card again and wondered why Officer Caldwell hadn't handed her his card when they met.

Officer Lincoln's uniform was black, not navy like Officer Caldwell's, and he was wearing his hat, which was broader and had a thick brim with a small band around it, not like the flat one with a bill that the first officer had carried under his arm.

Rose was puzzled. She didn't understand where Officer Caldwell had gone and she also didn't understand why the Oklahoma Highway Patrol wore different uniforms.

"Did Officer Caldwell get another call?" She turned to glance up toward the interstate.

"Who's Officer Caldwell?" the patrolman standing in front of her asked.

By this time, the second car had also pulled up beside her. There were two patrolmen in that car. Both of them quickly got out and came to stand with Officer Lincoln. They nodded at one another in acknowledgment. She suddenly felt surrounded.

"Patrolman Caldwell," she replied, remembering that she didn't know his first name. "He was the one just here." Feeling somewhat uncertain of the newly arrived threesome, she searched around her to see if she could make a run for it.

The three officers turned and looked at one another. They all shrugged.

"He said he got the call off the scanner and that he was a couple of exits down, not too far away on the interstate," she reported, retreating a bit, realizing the only thing she could do as a means of escape was to run to the highway.

"I was just dispatched to this location. I'm the first respondent," Officer Lincoln said. Then he nodded in the direction of the other two men, "This is Officer

Wallace, and that's Officer Patrick. They're the backup unit," he added. "We're all there is."

Rose stared down at the card she had been given. Then the other two men also handed her business cards with their names and information. She peered up at their uniforms, noticing the identification badges, both with photos of them clearly visible.

"This man was driving a dark SUV," Rose reported.

Then she thought about that. "Do Oklahoma patrolmen drive SUVs?" she asked.

"Not near here," the first officer said. "Mostly just out in the country."

"What did he say to you?" Officer Patrick asked. He was standing next to Officer Lincoln. The other patrolman had left the group and was walking around the camper.

Rose carefully watched the officer as he inspected the vehicle.

"He said he was Highway Patrol," she answered, feeling very confused. At that point, she didn't know whom to trust, and she tried to keep her eyes on all three patrolmen, especially the one who was moving around the camper. She turned to notice their cars. Both vehicles appeared much more official than the SUV. They were clearly designated as Oklahoma Highway Patrol and had lights attached to their roofs.

"Did he say anything else, try to get you to go with him?" It was Officer Patrick who asked this question. He seemed to be the youngest of the three. He was red-faced, freckled, had an innocence about him that softened Rose.

All three officers were now standing in front of her.

"He just wanted me to go in the camper to get—" Since she still wasn't sure which officer was the real officer, she didn't know if she should finish the statement. "To go in the camper" was all she said.

"And what happened then?" asked Officer Lincoln. He appeared to be about fifty and was the eldest of the three. He seemed to be in charge. The other two followed his lead.

"And then when I came out, he was gone. And you were driving up."

The three patrolmen turned to one another again, as if they knew one another's thoughts.

"Can you give a description of the guy?" Officer Lincoln asked.

And for this question, she was ready. "He was about thirty, had sandy brown hair that was cut real short and had a little curl on the top." Rose demonstrated with her finger in her hair. "He was about six feet tall, wore sunglasses—Ray-Bans, I think. His uniform was just like yours except it was navy blue and it was cut to fit tight across his chest. He had a gun, handcuffs, even a badge," she replied, thinking she'd done well to remember everything she had.

"Sounds like a fine-looking guy," Officer Wallace remarked, and smiled.

Rose blushed, realizing she had given a description that was just a bit too detailed.

"Did he have an identification card with his picture on it, his shield number?" asked Officer Patrick, the one with the freckles.

"No, just a badge," she answered, understanding that she should have known to ask for a photo ID. Her father would have really let her have it for that rookie mistake.

With that answer, all three nodded. Officer Lincoln walked over to his car and told the dispatcher what Rose had reported. In addition to the situation at the rest stop, as called in from a lawman in Arkansas, he noted, they were now in pursuit of a man driving a dark SUV, pretending to be a Highway Patrol officer.

"Ma'am," Officer Patrick said as they waited for the other man to return, "I don't think the guy you spoke to was a patrolman. I imagine he was hanging out somewhere close by and heard the police scanner. Lots of people have them," he explained. "He heard the report and knew you were out here alone." He cleared his throat. "There're a lot of sick people out there," he added.

Rose thought about the implication. If what they suspected was true, then Officer Caldwell, or whatever his name was, had simply chosen her as a target because it was reported that a woman was alone at the rest stop. At first, the possible scenario frightened her, but then she remembered the questions that he had asked, how interested he'd been in her situation. She recalled especially the question he had asked about what was in the trailer.

Somehow, she knew that Officer Caldwell was not just a predator looking for a target. Officer Caldwell was specifically interested in something in that trailer—namely, the ladder.

She remembered how excited he had gotten when she had mentioned the ladder to him, how he'd quickly moved to the camper and had her go inside to get it. When Rose replayed the event in her mind, she recognized that she had once again escaped from real danger.

As she continued to think about it, she began to wonder about the ladder and why it was of such interest. Once she realized that the ladder was somehow the key to everything that had happened over the last day or so, she couldn't wait to get a better look at it. She was quite curious as to why such an insignificant thing could be the motive behind murder, kidnapping, stealing, and now impersonating a police officer.

"Why don't you go sit in the car with Officer Patrick and give your statement. We'll take a good look around the vehicle and around the perimeter of the rest stop to see what we can find."

Officer Lincoln nodded toward the youngest patrolman, who waited for Rose and then started walking toward his car.

Rose followed him to the clearly marked Highway Patrol car and got in the passenger's side after he opened the door for her. She sat down and watched as the other two officers examined the outside of the truck and the camper. Officer Patrick walked around to the driver's side and got in beside her.

"Okay," he said as he got some papers together and retrieved a pen from the console in the car. "Let's start at the beginning. What are you doing in Checotah, Oklahoma, in a camper with New Mexico plates that was stolen in West Memphis, Arkansas?"

Rose sat back in her seat and began. She told the story very clearly and in great detail. Twenty minutes later, having failed to mention the bracelet in her front pocket and the ladder, which she now understood was the key to everything that had happened, Rose was given a cup of coffee from the vending machine, a pack of crackers, and was driven by Officer Lincoln to the station in Checotah, Oklahoma.

The morning was beginning to fade. Rose sat at a desk in the unfamiliar office.

It was four hours before Sheriff Montgomery arrived, and it would be after dark before she was back in her own camper at Shady Grove.

SEVENTEEN

Neither Rose nor the sheriff spoke a word until he drove across the border into Arkansas. Rose was tired and embarrassed about the way things had turned out; the lawman just wanted to get home.

Once he'd arrived in Checotah about 11:30 A.M.,

Sheriff Montgomery spent an hour with the Highway Patrol officer going over the event. Then he and Officer Lincoln drove Rose to Henryetta to the police station and then to the interstate, where she was able to identify the motel where the camper had been parked.

By the time they checked the place, about seven hours after she had escaped, there were no clues that the camper and the two men, whom she had heard but not seen, had ever been there.

The manager of the motel showed them the only room that had been rented between midnight and 6:00 A.M. It was on the end, right beside the office, room number 101, one of the rooms where they always put the late-night check-ins. He said it was a trucker who'd come in, a man by the name of Joe Lawson. A guy from Georgia, he stayed there regularly on his cross-country hauls.

The manager noted that they had rented fifteen of the forty rooms the previous night but that all of the guests except Mr. Lawson had gotten in before the other manager's shift ended at 11:00 P.M. He pulled out the files to verify what he'd said.

This employee, who had been on duty all night and was just about to go home, also showed the police the registration card of the Georgia resident, stamped at 5:20 A.M. Rose figured this person was the driver of the truck who had pulled up next to her when she had first awakened in the storage compartment of the trailer.

"No other check-ins," the manager said when Patrolman Lincoln asked again. "I'm sure."

Sheriff Montgomery turned to Rose and asked the question that she knew all of the other officers were thinking. "Are you sure this is the place?"

Rose could tell how it looked. She knew it was unlikely that two men would have stolen a camper, driven only a few hours after making the heist, and then pulled into a motel to get some sleep. And even if that story was as she'd reported, Rose understood the next puzzling question: If they hadn't stayed at the motel, where had they gone?

The manager certainly didn't appear to be lying about the one room that had been rented in the early hours of the morning; so, like everyone else, she wondered why the thieves had parked in the motel parking lot, gotten out, and then not gone into the motel.

She glanced around and noticed a gas station, a couple of fast-food restaurants—the places she remembered had been near the exit—but there was not much else around.

"Yeah, I know this is it. I remember the parking lot," she told them. Then she thought for a second.

Rose was trying to imagine possible scenarios. "Maybe they just stopped here and had somebody pick them up."

One of the police officers from Henryetta twirled a toothpick in his mouth, sliding it from side to side. He was tall, skinny, and had acted perturbed the whole time they had been at the motel. He turned to Rose, raising an eyebrow. He folded his arms across his chest, relaxing his stance. "You sure you didn't drive that camper to Henryetta yourself?" he asked, his voice smacking of contempt.

Rose felt her face redden. Of course that's what the two lawmen from Henryetta would think. The one who asked the question was grinning at her like he had caught her in a lie and the other one, appearing somewhat bored with the entire situation, had returned to his car.

That's what the patrolmen from Checotah must think, too, she realized as they walked away from the conversation, whispering to themselves. And when she turned to Sheriff Montgomery, his eyes quickly darted away from hers and his head jerked toward the interstate. She knew that he thought the same thing, too. His lack of support was devastating.

A deputy from West Memphis was dispatched to pick up the rig from the Highway Patrol office in Oklahoma. They still needed it for the murder investigation. He was already on his way when Sheriff Montgomery and Rose left for home.

Before they got ready to leave, she thought about the ladder, considered telling the sheriff or the Highway Patrol officers about it before they departed, about the impersonating officer who seemed to know of it. But she was so troubled about being disbelieved, so hurt by the way Sheriff Montgomery had turned away from her, she offered no further comments. She could not bring herself to introduce anything else to the group of men assigned to sort through her adventure.

She sat in the passenger's seat of the sheriff's car and did not speak a word as they drove away. She stared out the window at the sights they sped past, counted the exits, and, only to herself, named the birds that rested on fence posts and darted across the golden fields beside the interstate. She rode along silently, not knowing anything to say.

Finally, once they crossed into Arkansas, the sheriff made an attempt at conversation. "You get anything to eat today?" he asked.

Rose was hungry, but she didn't want to make the trip to West Memphis any longer than it had to be.

"I had something this morning," she told him, noticing the clock on the dashboard. It was after 3:00 P.M. Neither of them had eaten lunch.

"There's a place up the road in Russellville," he replied. "Burgers mostly, but it's not bad."

Rose made no response.

They drove a few more miles. He turned off the exit and into the parking lot of a diner. It was empty except for only a couple of vehicles. Staff, Rose assumed. They got out of the car and went in.

It wasn't until they sat down in a booth, had given their orders, and were facing each other with uncomfortable looks that Rose took the bracelet out of her pocket and placed it on the table between them.

"That's why I was at the camper," she suddenly

confessed, pushing the bracelet toward the sheriff. "I found it yesterday morning after I realized the man was dead. It was out in the grass, next to his truck."

The sheriff picked up the piece of jewelry and turned it over in his hands.

The waitress arrived with their drinks and Rose waited until the woman had gone before continuing.

"I don't know why I kept it," she said. "I just did. I took it to the library after I left your office, tried to figure out what the symbols are; then I was going to take it back and drop it off in the grass again, where I found it to begin with."

The sheriff had pulled his reading glasses out of his shirt pocket and was studying it. He still did not respond.

"I waited until late, about midnight, to return it. And that's why I was there," she said.

Sheriff Montgomery looked up at Rose, peering at her over his glasses. There was a long pause.

"I didn't steal the camper and drive it to Oklahoma," she said. She was weary of the silence. "It's like I told you on the phone, I heard the men come up from the river and I hid inside. I had no idea what they were going to do. Then they pulled out."

She wiped her hands on the tops of her legs. "I hid in the storage compartment and then I fell asleep."

A couple of men walked into the diner and Rose glanced up before going on. They sat down at a booth on the other side of the room. She thought nothing of it.

"When I woke up, we were no longer moving, and the men were gone. That's when I found the extra keys and drove away." She took a swallow of her drink.

She waited for the sheriff to say something.

"I didn't make it up," she said. "I didn't steal the camper and drive to Oklahoma."

The waitress brought over their food. Sheriff Montgomery slid the bracelet off the table and held it in his lap. They both said that everything looked fine when they were asked about their orders, then waited until she left again.

"Why didn't you show me this before?" he finally asked, referring to the bracelet. He took off his glasses and stuck them in his pocket.

Rose reached for the salt and added some to her french fries. She shrugged her shoulders like a teenager in trouble, then took a bite.

"I don't know," she said truthfully, her mouth full of food.

Sheriff Montgomery slipped the bracelet in with his glasses and began eating his lunch.

Rose waited for him to ask another question, but he didn't say anything else until he had finished eating his hamburger. Then he drank all of his soda and wiped his mouth.

"I don't think you stole the camper," he finally said.

Rose turned away. She was still eating her food. She noticed one of the two men in the booth sitting across from her peer in her direction. For a moment, she thought there was something familiar about him, but she quickly turned to face the sheriff.

"Is there anything else you haven't told me?" he asked.

"There was a secret area," she said, sliding her plate away from her, having eaten all she wanted. "Someone modified the storage compartment under the bed, made a fake wall and a hidden area in the rear."

The sheriff was listening closely.

"I fell through the fake wall," she reported.

The waitress returned to the table and cleared away the plates. Neither of them wanted dessert, so she left the bill with Sheriff Montgomery.

"I didn't think anything about it at first, but later, when the first officer who wasn't really an officer—" She stopped abruptly, wondering if she needed to explain, but then realized by the nod of his head that the sheriff knew about the impersonator.

"When he asked me if I had found anything odd inside the camper, I mentioned the ladder." Rose took a drink of water. "Well, now I think that may be what the killers were after in the first place."

Sheriff Montgomery appeared puzzled. "A hidden compartment?" he asked, not sure of what she meant.

"No, the ladder." She waited. "That's what was in the hidden compartment. I fell on it," she added.

"The man from New Mexico had made a special compartment, hidden under his bed, for a ladder?" he asked, considering this new information.

Rose nodded and then shrugged her shoulders again. "I know, it seems weird to me, too. And I never really saw it. It was dark when I was on top of it, and when I went inside to get it for the officer who wasn't really an officer, I still couldn't see anything then, either."

Sheriff Montgomery seemed to be deliberating about what Rose was saying. He pulled out the bracelet and then put on his reading glasses, studying it again. He rolled it around in his hands and then he pointed to one of the signs. It was one that Rose hadn't been able to identify, but as he turned and showed it to her, she recognized what he had discovered. The symbol with the two parallel lines with small intersecting lines between them was a ladder. She was surprised she hadn't realized this at first.

"This one is a river." He pointed out three wavy lines. "And this one is the sign for death." Sheriff Montgomery showed Rose the one that was a darkened square.

She nodded. She had found that one in the book at the library.

"I think this one has to do with talking to spirits, and if I remember my petroglyphs," he said, holding the jewelry very close to his eyes, "this one stands for evil."

Rose noticed the one he was referring to. It was a circle, half darkened, half decorated with small dots. She hadn't known that one, either. She knew the symbol for the kiva and the one for the sun.

Sheriff Montgomery was still studying the bracelet when the man from the other booth, the one who had been sitting on the side facing Rose, walked by them. He glimpsed down and Rose saw that he noticed the jewelry that the sheriff was handling.

The man headed in the direction of the rest rooms. Rose felt a strange sensation when he passed her, as if she had seen him before. She suddenly became anxious.

"Let's go home," she said to Sheriff Montgomery, getting up from her seat. Since she had already been wrong about so many things, she didn't want to say anything about her suspicion of the man. She also, however, didn't want to hang around.

"Okay, but I need to use the facilities," he replied, placing the bracelet back in his pocket.

Rose sat down again, trying to tell herself that she was just being oversensitive. She watched as the sheriff went to the rest room, following the man who had just walked by.

She waited a few minutes, growing more and more nervous, wondering what was happening in the men's rest room. Finally, just before she was about to go and knock on the door where she knew they both were, the sheriff returned.

"Okay, to West Memphis," he said, patting himself on the belly and walking toward the register to pay the bill.

Rose peered behind them in the direction from which the sheriff had come. There was no one following him, and when she turned back to the booth where the two men had been sitting, it was completely empty.

After the sheriff paid the bill, she followed him out the door and got into the car.

EIGHTEEN

I heard about your ex-husband," Sheriff Montgomery said as they pulled out of the parking lot.

Rose was searching all around, trying to find the two men who had come into the diner after they had. There was no sign of them anywhere. They weren't in the parking lot or anywhere on the road. She knew she would recognize only the one who had walked past them, and even then, she wasn't completely sure she'd gotten a good look at him.

"How did you find out about that?" she asked, wondering how the story about her ex-husband's visit had gotten around town so fast.

"Mary," he said.

He made the turn down the ramp, heading east on the interstate. He merged into the right lane.

"I called the campground office before I left this morning. I thought they might be worried about you when you didn't show up for work."

Rose nodded. She was glad that he had thought of that. She knew that they would have been concerned when she didn't appear at the office for her shift.

They would have searched her camper, bothered all the guests about her whereabouts. She considered the sheriff's action to be a very generous one.

"She said that you were pretty upset about him coming to find you." He turned to peer at Rose, as if he was searching for something.

She didn't really understand what he was getting at.

"Yeah, well, it was a shock," she replied, remembering how unsettled she had been only twenty-four hours earlier. She had forgotten all that had happened at Shady Grove once she had been hijacked to Oklahoma.

Then once she answered with those words, she recognized the sheriff's line of questioning. "So, you think that's it?" she asked, surprised and angry that he had made such assumptions about her, especially after the confession she had given at the diner. "You think I was upset because Rip showed up? You think I was somehow distraught in such a way that I waited until midnight and then stole a dead man's camper?"

The sheriff drove along carefully in the traffic. He started to excuse his behavior and then admitted she was right.

"Yes, once we left Henryetta, at first," he replied. "When there was no evidence of anybody at the motel, yes, that's what I thought."

Rose turned away. She suddenly regretted having given him the bracelet.

"But I don't think that now," he said, trying to soothe things between them. "I think you're telling

168

the truth," he added, his voice somewhat apologetic.

Rose hesitated before speaking. She realized he was trying to make amends. And yet, in spite of his intentions, she wasn't quite ready to forgive him.

The interstate was getting more crowded with cars. It was growing late, and as they got closer to the state capital, it was obvious that lots of people were going home from work. She watched the cars pass, thinking about where they would be returning. She wondered how many of them were happy to be going home and how many of them were dissatisfied with their lives.

"What did he want?" the sheriff asked. "I mean, if you don't mind me asking," he added.

Rose remembered the conversation with Rip. She didn't really have any reason not to tell anybody, although she realized she hadn't mentioned their conversation to Mary or Ms. Lou Ellen after he left. Once she thought about it, she figured the lawman would find out anyway. "He came to tell me my father is dying and that I should go home to see him."

The sheriff didn't respond. It was clearly a more intimate subject than he'd expected. He suddenly seemed uncomfortable.

"You have any children?" she asked. Now that she had been pressured to share all of her secrets with the sheriff, she felt like talking, and since he was asking personal questions, she thought she was entitled, as well. She was, after all, curious about the sheriff from West Memphis, Arkansas.

He shook his head and turned to look out his window.

"I was married once," he said.

"Yeah? She get tired of your line of work and leave you for a banker?" She meant it to be funny.

"No. Actually, he was a traveling salesman," the sheriff responded, leaving Rose feeling slightly embarrassed. "I guess she liked what he was selling," he added, not appearing angry about her implication.

"I'm sorry," Rose said. "I didn't know," she added, trying to make up for her insensitive remark.

"It's okay," he replied. "It was a long time ago." He turned to Rose, who was facing him. "I wasn't a great husband," he confessed. "I had it coming."

Rose didn't know what else to say. Now she was the one who was suddenly uncomfortable with her questions and his answers.

"So, you got divorced?" he asked.

Rose nodded. "Yep, he wasn't such a great husband, either," she noted. "And I didn't leave for a traveling salesman; he left me."

They drove along in traffic.

"But it's for the best," she continued. "The truth is, we weren't really a good match." She thought about what she was saying. "It's funny what you think will make you happy when you're young, what you think you've got to have."

The sheriff appeared to consider what Rose was saying. He smiled and nodded.

"I married Rip to get away from my father," Rose explained. "That and the fact that I thought nobody else would ever ask me."

"I guess most people get married for a few wrong reasons," he said as he wove in and out of the cars around them. "Fear, selfishness, boredom. But in the end, you just hope the right reason will win out."

Rose thought about this, remembering how she had felt when she got married, how glad she was to be on her own, starting her own family, disconnecting herself from the one she had been raised in. She thought about Rip, how good-looking he was, how fortunate she'd felt at the time that he had picked her. She knew she had married him for some desperate reasons, but she also knew that she loved him. Even though she hadn't really known what it meant at the time, she understood, years later, that in the only way she knew how, she loved him.

"You never married again?" she asked, feeling a bit relieved of the anger and disappointment she had felt earlier in the drive.

The sheriff shook his head. "Nah," he said. "I'm way too ornery now. Too much negotiating in a marriage. I'm afraid I lost those skills when I picked this line of duty."

Rose laughed.

"You, on the other hand, seemed to have recovered," he observed. "What's the status with you and Mr. Sawyer these days?"

"You're a little more than nosy, don't you think?" she said, only teasing. "It's uncomplicated. And for now, that's more than enough."

The sheriff nodded as if he understood.

They drove a bit farther without conversation, both of them glad for what had emerged between them. Rose realized that she hadn't been completely fair with him, that once given the opportunity, the sheriff of West Memphis was actually a decent guy.

They headed out of Little Rock and the evening commute and drove eastward into Prairie County. The sun was low in the sky and the sheriff reached up and turned up the heat.

"Did you get in trouble with the FBI?" Rose asked, grateful for the warmth. She remembered the phone call Mary had received. She also remembered that the agent was supposed to have come by the campground earlier that day.

"Why would I be in trouble with the FBI?" he asked.

"The guy who called said he was going to inspect the camper this morning. He called Shady Grove to tell Mary."

"I don't know anything about the Bureau being involved in this," he said.

Rose noticed that Sheriff Montgomery kept watching out his rearview mirror. She turned around in her seat to see behind the car.

"What's wrong?" she asked, not noticing anything peculiar. There were a few cars traveling behind them.

"Nothing," the sheriff said, still glancing in the mirror.

Rose turned around again. This time, she saw a car

speed up behind them as if it were going to pass and then fall away once the sheriff slowed down.

"They've been back there since Russellville," he said, realizing that Rose now saw the car. "Maybe just coincidence," he added.

Rose remembered the two men in the booth. "Was there a man in the rest room at the diner?" she asked, now feeling comfortable sharing her concerns.

The sheriff seemed to think about the question. "I didn't see anybody," he said. "But that doesn't mean there wasn't somebody in one of the stalls," he added, remembering a closed door. "Why, did you see something?"

"Well, a guy walked past us and went in there before you did. He saw the bracelet." Rose turned around again to look at the cars behind them. The one she had seen before was now pulling up beside them. Just as it was about to slow up and pull behind the patrol car as it had done earlier, Sheriff Montgomery took his foot off of the accelerator and the car went past.

Rose noticed right away that there were two men in the front seat, that it was an old sedan, and that the plates were from New Mexico. Just as they drove past, the car moved into the right lane, in front of Sheriff Montgomery, and the driver quickly stepped on the brakes.

The patrol car swerved onto the right shoulder, barely missing the car that had been following them, the one that had jumped in front and stopped.

Sheriff Montgomery slid to an abrupt stop, the front of the car landing in a ditch, the frame now bent and smashed against the tire. He yelled at Rose to get down, then jumped out of the driver's side, his gun raised, aimed, and ready to fire.

NINETEEN

Get out of the car with your hands up!" the sheriff yelled.

Rose was down on the floor of the front seat, her arms over her head. She waited for gunfire or some kind of commotion to begin outside. She felt around her head and neck, touching herself just to make sure everything was still intact. She had been thrown against the door when the sheriff swerved, slamming her head against the window. When she reached up, she felt a bit of blood trickling down her forehead.

She turned to her left and saw Sheriff Montgomery squatting behind the open door on the driver's side. Rose quickly noticed that he had his gun pulled and aimed around his door at the car in front of them. She couldn't see what else was happening.

In only a few seconds, however, the sheriff stood up and began walking away from the car. Since no bullets had been fired, she assumed the men in the car were obeying his command. She remained in her protected position. More time passed. She couldn't hear what was going on outside the car.

Finally, after more than a few minutes, Rose became unable to control her curiosity. She carefully lifted herself up and peeked over the dashboard of the car. When she did, she saw the sheriff checking the identification of both the driver and his passenger, his gun still pointed in their direction.

Both men were out of the car, arms held high, fingers interlocked and resting behind their heads. They were facing away from Sheriff Montgomery, legs spread, leaning against the front of their car. Rose opened the door and emerged from her place on the floor. The sheriff turned to her quickly.

"Stay in there," he instructed her, in a commanding tone. He noticed the blood on her face right away.

She quickly returned to her seat, watching the interaction between Sheriff Montgomery and the older of the two men. He had turned his head around, his eyes facing to the side, and appeared to be answering the lawman's questions. The young one was quietly leaning against the car. Rose could see his right leg was shaking.

She opened the glove compartment and found a couple of napkins and began to apply pressure to her head wound. She felt a slight ache just above her eyes; but even as she wiped away the blood, she continued to watch what was going on in front of her.

It wasn't long before she could tell these men meant no harm. It was clear in how nervous and obedient they were, how small they seemed next to the sheriff. She didn't know why they had almost caused the wreck with the patrol car, but it appeared to her that it wasn't because they intended to hurt the sheriff or his passenger.

It was also clear to Rose that these were not the two men she had seen at the diner. Even though she couldn't identify either of the men who had sat near her, she remembered that those two were more sure of themselves, had an air of cockiness about them that she had spotted once they walked in the door.

She also recalled that the one who had gone past them, the one who had seen the bracelet, was taller than both of these men, and better dressed, too.

This pair, she later found out, had indeed been following the sheriff and Rose, but they had been following because they too were on their way to West Memphis.

These two were John and Daniel Sunspeaker from Gallup, New Mexico. They were father and son, relatives of Jacob Sunspeaker, the man who had been killed at Shady Grove.

When they pulled out from the gas station and saw the West Memphis sheriff's patrol car just ahead of them, they had tried to catch up with it and get the attention of the driver. They hurried all the way through Little Rock and on into Lonoke and Carlisle, never quite being able to catch them because of the traffic and the highly unreliable engine of the sedan they were driving.

Finally, having passed the sheriff, Mr. Sunspeaker decided to pull off the road and wave down the patrol car. Unfortunately, with the setting sun reflecting in his rearview mirror, he hadn't realized how close the car was behind him and hadn't taken into account the danger he could create by pulling in front and then slamming on his brakes. He also didn't know the trouble he was in until Sheriff Montgomery jumped from the car with his pistol aimed and ready to shoot.

When Rose saw the sheriff talking to them, both men now turned and faced him, their hands down at their sides, she moved from her seat and walked over to the three men. This time, the sheriff did not order her to the car.

"You okay?" He knew she had been hurt in the accident.

She nodded. "Just a bit of a headache," she replied.

"Show me," he instructed.

Rose pulled away the napkin and displayed a raised knot about the size of child's fist just above her right eye. A cut across her brow was bleeding, but only slightly.

"I'm so sorry," the man who had been driving said. "I didn't know you were that close behind me."

"It's okay. It's nothing really," she said, putting the napkin over the wound and smiling to show that she was fine.

"This is the nephew of . . ." the sheriff hesitated. "This is John Sunspeaker," he then said.

Rose nodded at the older of the two men. She remembered having heard the murder victim's name from the man who had called Mary at Shady Grove, the man who said he was a FBI agent.

"His son," Sheriff Montgomery added, "Daniel."

"Rose Franklin," she said, placing the napkin in her left hand and reaching out with her right.

John Sunspeaker was middle-aged. He was of medium stature, had a round face, dark complexion, and long black hair that was tied with a leather string behind his back. He was wearing a dark T-shirt, blue jeans, and a pair of old running shoes.

His son, Daniel, looked to be in his early twenties, maybe even still a teenager. Rose couldn't tell for sure. Like his father, he was not very tall, either, and he seemed uncomfortable standing on the side of the road with a sheriff beside him. He was also dressed in jeans and a T-shirt, but his hair was close-cropped, he was gangly, and his arms were long and tan.

Rose noticed that the older of the two men was wearing a bracelet, similar to the cuff-style one she had found and given to the sheriff. She tried to see the designs on his, but he quickly reached over, covering it with his other hand.

"I'm sorry we frightened you," the driver, John, said to Rose.

"Yeah, well, I'm sorry he frightened you," she replied, referring to the sheriff with his drawn weapon.

When Sheriff Montgomery heard that, he placed his pistol back in the holster attached to his belt and placed his hands on his hips.

"I was telling the sheriff that we saw you leave Russellville. I've been trying to catch up with you since then." Mr. Sunspeaker was putting his driver's license back in his wallet. "We just got called last night about my mother's oldest brother," he said, not referring to the dead man by name. "I noticed your car and thought we could follow you into the town where it happened." He hesitated. "Where he is," he added softly.

Rose nodded. She did not think she was owed an explanation. "I'm afraid I caused you to wreck your car," he said. "I meant no danger."

"Well," the sheriff replied, turning to get a view of his damaged car, the right side hanging low on the soft shoulder. "We were fortunate we didn't slam into you." He eyed the side of the road where he had found enough room to swerve away from hitting the man's car. After noticing the damage to the vehicle's right side, he shook his head, unsure of whether or not the car could be pulled out of the narrow ditch and driven back to his office.

The other three followed his eyes and all of them saw the bent piece, the drag of the frame against the tire, the angle of the car's front end where it was lodged in the ditch.

Rose glanced up at the sky. It was getting dark. She suddenly wished she had some aspirin, as her head was starting to throb.

As if the older man had read her thoughts, he turned to his son, and, speaking in a language Rose had never heard, instructed him to get something from the car. The younger man started to open the car door and then glanced over at the sheriff, his face a question mark.

Understanding what the young man was asking, Sheriff Montgomery raised both of his hands as a gesture of release. He saw no reason to detain them or to distrust them. He thought their story was believable.

With permission given, the young man opened the back door and reached across the seat. He brought out a canvas bag and gave it to his father.

"Something for your wound," Mr. Sunspeaker said, pulling out a square piece of material that was wrapped in a paper bag. Rose smelled it as he reached up to place it against her forehead. It reminded her of the forest, like the leaves of old trees.

He gently pressed it against the knot on her head and the pressure of his hand on the swelling caused her to retreat.

"I'm sorry," he said, stepping away, almost dropping the cloth.

She reached up, holding the dressing in place. "It's okay," she said. The piece of material felt cool against her head.

"Why don't you sit down in the car," the sheriff said. "We can work on the bumper and pull the frame away from the tire and maybe I can get us home." Then he studied Rose. "Or should I call for an ambulance?" he asked, examining her head very closely.

"No," she responded. "It's just a bump, no concussion. I can recite all the presidents, if you want." She faced the sheriff with a smile, clearly displaying her wound. He agreed it didn't appear too serious.

"I'll just sit in the car and wait," she said, heading toward the sheriff's car.

"Here, sit in ours," Mr. Sunspeaker said. He spoke again to his son in the language only they understood, and then both of them began clearing away their belongings on the backseat. Each of them took an armful of clothes and assorted containers and placed them in the trunk. When they had made a place for her to sit, Rose smiled again, walked over to the car, leaned inside, and sat down. She was glad to get off of her feet, because she was feeling a little dizzy.

She didn't turn around, but she could tell from the sounds of physical exertion and the instructions the sheriff was barking out that they were trying to pull the bent right piece of the frame away from the tire and get the car out of the ditch. It took almost an hour before the three men returned to the car where Rose was sitting.

"Okay," the sheriff said, checking closely on Rose. "I think we're good to go."

She slowly got out of the other car with the sheriff's help. "Great," she said, and headed to the patrol car.

Mr. Sunspeaker walked beside her and opened the passenger's door.

"Thank you," she said, sliding in and then pulling the seat belt around her.

He replied with a nod. Then he closed the door and

headed to his car. His son had already gotten in and the sheriff was waiting at the driver's side.

"We have about two more hours to go," he reported to Mr. Sunspeaker. "You can just follow us on into town. I'll take you to the local hotel," he added.

The older man nodded, opened his door, and got in.

When the sheriff started his engine, he slowly pulled his car away from the ditch. The driver of the other car waited until the patrol car merged onto the interstate and then he pulled in behind him.

It was well after 9:00 P.M. before the sheriff drove into Shady Grove and let Rose out at the cabin by the office. He quickly jumped to her side of the car, opened her door, and left only when he was sure there was someone at Ms. Lou Ellen's house to take care of her.

He waved good-bye and pulled out of Shady Grove as the Boyds, Mary, Thomas, Ms. Lou Ellen, and a dog all poured onto the front porch.

TWENTY

Lucas was the one to come down the steps first. "Oh, little sister."

Rose glanced up when the sheriff pulled away and saw her friends join Lucas at the front door. The three-legged dog stood near Ms. Lou Ellen's feet.

"What on earth happened?" Rhonda asked. They could all see the gash on her forehead and they all ran down the stairs to get to her.

"He do this to you?" Mary was holding her by the arm and pulling her up the steps. She peered up the driveway at the sheriff's car exiting.

"No," Rose said, and then everyone began asking her questions. "Are you okay?" "Where have you been?" "How did you get hurt?" She was unable to answer them all.

She noticed Tom right away. She smiled at him and was glad to feel his arms around her. Even though he had only been gone couple of days, it felt like months since she had seen him. She had so much she needed to talk to him about.

"We had a little wreck on the way back," she explained.

"Dear, we thought you were dead." Ms. Lou Ellen remained standing in the doorway. There was an edge to her voice, a raised tone that Rose had not heard before. The three-legged dog began to bark.

"Yes, Lester Earl," she said to the dog, trying to sound cheerful. "It is Rose and she appears to be alive." They both moved aside as the group walked inside.

When Rose entered the cabin, relieved to be at Shady Grove, she immediately noticed an assortment of dishes spread across the kitchen table. There were a couple of cakes, several casseroles, two bowls of salad. She looked around, lifting her nose in the air, smelling all sorts of aromas, but she was confused about what she saw. She glanced into the kitchen, only to find even more food covering every inch of space available.

"Did you have a big dinner?" she asked, surprised at the amount of food, especially at such a late hour.

Mary rolled her eyes and moved near the table. Rhonda and Lucas followed her, waiting for Ms. Lou Ellen to explain.

She hesitated at first while Rose and Thomas sat down on her sofa.

"First of all," the older woman replied, realizing they were all waiting for her to explain why there was so much food, "we all need to hear from Rose."

She cleared her throat and turned to her friend. "Dear, are you all right?"

They all listened carefully for her answer.

"I'm fine," she responded. "I just banged my head against the window. I have a headache is all." She rested against Thomas's shoulder.

"Let me find you an aspirin," Rhonda said, hurrying into the back of the house.

"We were really worried about you," Thomas said, checking her forehead.

"We hadn't heard anything else about you since the sheriff called this morning to tell us you were kidnapped," Lucas said as he sat at the table.

He leaned very near to her and Rose could see the concern in his eyes. She guessed that he had been praying all day and she waited for him to offer up some prayer of thanksgiving right then, but he just watched her.

Rhonda returned with a bottle of pills. She went over to the sink and poured Rose a glass of water.

"Who kidnap you?" Mary asked as she stood behind the table.

"Here." Rhonda handed Rose the pills and a drink.

"I don't know," Rose replied, taking a couple of aspirin and a sip of water.

Rhonda sat down beside Lucas and the two of them did bow their heads for a moment. Out of respect, Rose waited before she went on with her story. When they raised up, smiles on their faces, she continued.

"I was out at the dead man's camper." She turned to Ms. Lou Ellen, as if the older woman would understand. Ms. Lou Ellen quickly turned away. The news had a noticeable effect on her.

Everyone witnessed the exchange between the two women; however, neither Rose nor Ms. Lou Ellen elaborated.

"It was really late," she went on, "about midnight. And I heard some men come up from the river. I got scared and jumped in the camper. Then the next thing I knew, they drove off. I'm not sure how long we rode, because I got sleepy. But when I woke up, we had stopped in Henryetta." She took a breath.

"When I got out of the camper, they were gone. I was able to find keys to the truck and drive it back to Checotah. Then the police came, and then Sheriff Montgomery, and I've been with him every since."

She exhaled, exhausted from repeating the same story over so many times in one day.

The group was silent.

"When we were driving home, the dead man's

185

nephew ran us off the road. That was when we had the accident." She took another sip of water.

This part brought more questions from the group.

"How did the dead man's nephew find you on the highway?" Rhonda asked.

Rose shrugged. "Just a weird coincidence, I think," she replied. "He had been called about his relative and was on his way here to take care of things. He saw the patrol car with West Memphis written on it when we had stopped for something to eat in Russellville. He followed us and tried to get Sheriff Montgomery's attention."

"So he ran you off the road?" Thomas asked. "That seems a little over the top."

"He didn't mean to run us off the road," Rose replied. "It was an accident."

"What about the kidnappers?" Lucas asked.

Everyone leaned in for the answer.

Rose just shook her head. "We don't know," she said with more than a hint of disappointment in her voice. "They were gone by the time the police got there."

"In Henryetta?" asked Lucas.

Rose nodded. "At a motel."

"You never saw them?" Rhonda asked.

"No," Rose replied. "I hid inside a storage bin. I don't even think they knew I was in there."

The group was silent, thinking over everything she had reported.

Finally, Rhonda spoke the words everyone was

thinking. "We're just all glad you're home and okay."

"Me, too," Rose replied, grateful for the love of her friends.

Thomas squeezed her on the leg and there were a few moments of silence as everyone stared at Rose.

"So, why all the food?" Rose asked again.

Ms. Lou Ellen swept her hair behind her ear as everyone looked in her direction.

"When we heard the ghastly report from Sheriff Montgomery, I was beside myself with worry. We were all sure there would be more bad news."

"Okay," Rose said, waiting for the rest of the story. The fact that she had been given up for dead had already been established.

"And everybody knows a person loses her appetite upon hearing the devastating confirmation of the death of a loved one."

She sounded perfectly reasonable, and Rose was touched by being referred to as "a loved one." She smiled.

"So, when Mary here"—she nodded at her friend, who once again rolled her eyes at the older woman— "told me about the sheriff's call and your late-night mishap, I thought it was best to make sure we all ate before we were struck anorexic with the later report of your violent death."

Rose crossed her brows in her confusion, suddenly feeling the ache of her wound. The story had suddenly gone in a direction she was no longer following.

"Mama's been cooking since dawn," Rhonda reported. "She wasn't going to stop until we heard what had happened to you."

"That's right, little sister," Lucas added.

"So, let me get this straight. You've just been eating all day so that when you got bad news and you couldn't eat, you'd already be full?" Rose asked, trying to make sure she understood what her friends were saying.

"I've been to the grocery store four times," Rhonda said.

"She asked me to go only an hour ago," Thomas reported.

"I never know her to eat so much," Mary said. "She and that dog eat all day."

"I do believe there were more than just two plates to be washed at dinnertime," Ms. Lou Ellen said, implicating the others in the room.

They all turned away.

"And you just kept cooking?" Rose asked, still surprised by the way her friend responded to bad news.

"When the hours passed, Rose," Ms. Lou Ellen explained as she sat down at the table next to her daughter, "I began to think about the funeral event and how there would be the necessity for a large gathering of friends and family." She winked at Tom when she said the word *family*.

He smiled in return.

"And I knew there would be a need for vast variety," she continued.

"Even though the grief would have taken away everyone's appetite?" Rose asked.

The older woman seemed indignant at the question. "Rose, you above all people understand that you cannot die in the South without proper dietary arrangements," Ms. Lou Ellen responded. "Whether the bereaved eats or chooses not to eat, someone is responsible for providing the opportunity for selection. There must be casseroles present."

To hear the explanation, Rose thought, it sounded perfectly rational. "So, you've been cooking funeral food all day?"

"Anticipatory grief food," Ms. Lou Ellen replied, "until about noon; then it was funeral food." She folded her hands in her lap.

"Little sister, we have been worried sick," Lucas said. "Whereas I go to praying, my mother-in-law finds baking eases the tension of a long wait."

Rose looked at all the dishes spread across the table and the countertops, along the top of the refrigerator, and across the stove. She saw how much Ms. Lou Ellen had cooked and she suddenly understood that every dish represented an hour of impatient and anxious waiting. She was moved by her friend's concern.

"Well, since there will be no funeral anytime soon, not for me anyway," Rose said, trying to show her gratitude, "I think we should eat something now."

The sighs of everyone gathered around her surprised Rose. Obviously, they had already partaken of the funeral nourishment provided by Ms. Lou Ellen, or maybe it was the anticipatory grief food—Rose wasn't sure.

"We'd love to sit with you while you have a plate," Thomas said, speaking for everyone there. "But we're really full," he added.

"We have enough food now that we can grieve for everybody who will one day be dead," Mary said, standing up and heading into the kitchen.

"And that," Ms. Lou Ellen said as she stood up to get Rose a plate, appearing relieved, "is a very respectable thing."

Rose laughed and relaxed in her seat, waiting to be served.

TWENTY-ONE

Thomas walked Rose to her camper after she had sampled everything Ms. Lou Ellen had cooked and after everyone was convinced that she was really okay. It was late, and Rose was glad to be finding her way to her own bed once again. She was exhausted from all of the day's events. She held Thomas's hand as they strolled toward the river.

"Did you find a tractor?" she asked, remembering the reason for his trip to Fort Smith. They had not talked about his trip.

He nodded. "Found one first thing this morning," he told her.

They stopped at the picnic table closest to her

campsite. She eased down and he sat next to her.

"I got back here about ten," he said. "I stopped at the office first, to see you, and that was when Mary told me what had happened."

Rose listened as he explained.

"I've been crazy worried," he said. "We all have."

She leaned against him.

"I know," she said.

They sat in the silence of the late night.

"Lou Ellen was the most upset," he said. "She thought she was responsible for what happened because she was the one who told you to return the bracelet to the crime scene."

"You know about that?"

Thomas nodded. "In between cooking the entrées and the desserts, she confessed. She said that it had been her idea for you to be out there last night. She was so angry with herself for advising you to do that. She was more upset than I've ever seen her."

"So, it was more than just expecting bad news and preparing for a funeral that caused her to do all that cooking," Rose said.

"Yeah, I'd say guilt had as much to do with her Martha Stewart tendencies as concern or sadness."

Rose suddenly felt terrible for her friend. She then understood the unsettled look she had noticed on Ms. Lou Ellen when she first returned.

"It wasn't her fault," she said to Thomas, realizing that she would need to tell that to Ms. Lou Ellen, too.

"I know, and I told her the same thing. But she took it hard, the news of what happened to you. She even swore off sharing her ideas." Thomas smiled.

Rose was surprised. "She really was upset!" Then she thought about it. "Of course, that won't last."

"I know. By the end of the afternoon, she was already telling me about her idea of going into the catering business. She wanted me to be her partner. She drew up plans, figured out where she would advertise. She even came up with a company logo." Thomas shifted in his seat at the table. "She had several choices, but it turned out she was partial to the name Funeral Foodery."

"Foodery?" Rose asked. "Where did she get that?"

Thomas shook his head. "Who knows where our dear friend gets anything." He slid his arm around Rose.

"But she was upset that you had done what she had suggested and then gotten into such danger."

Rose nodded.

A late-night breeze blew across the river. They huddled closer together.

"I gave the bracelet to the sheriff," she told him. "I guess he'll give it to the nephew." She certainly hoped that he would.

"Lou Ellen said that you went to the library and that you were trying to figure out the symbols on it," Thomas said.

Rose nodded. "Yeah, and I didn't know it at the time, but the sheriff knew a lot of them." She remembered how quickly he'd identified the ones she hadn't been able to find.

"It was apparently something like a story bracelet. There were a lot of symbols engraved on it." She recalled what she had learned.

"There was one for death, one for evil, one for speaking to spirits, a river, and a ladder," she reported. And then she paused. "And actually, I think the murder has something to do with that one," she said. "The ladder, I mean."

Thomas turned to face her. "What makes you think that?" he asked.

"I found a ladder in the camper—in a little hidden compartment. Then a man showed up before the Highway Patrol, a man who claimed to be a patrolman and who actually turned out later not to be one, and he was really interested in it once I told him what I had found."

"There was a man pretending to be a police officer?" Thomas asked, not having heard this part of the story.

Rose nodded. "He came up just after I had called Sheriff Montgomery. He certainly dressed the part of patrolman, had me fooled. But then he drove away when the real Highway Patrol showed up."

Thomas thought about the new information and then he considered her theory. "What did the ladder look like?" he asked.

Rose shook her head. "I don't know. I never saw it because it was so dark inside. All I know is that it felt like wood and that there were studs along it, like stones or something."

She sat thinking about the things that had happened. "What I don't understand is why somebody would murder a person for a ladder."

"Must be a ladder worth some money," Thomas responded. "Greed is always a motive for homicide," he added.

They both remembered the murder that had occurred earlier that year, the one prompted by a report of gold coins and the misinformation that Thomas's friend Lawrence Franklin had them in his possession.

Rose tried to imagine what kind of ladder might be of value. Then she thought of the dead man's name. She mentioned it to Thomas.

"It's Jacob's ladder," she said.

"What?" He did not know the name of the deceased.

"The old man who was murdered. His name was Jacob. It was Jacob's ladder," she said again.

They both paused, thinking about her observation.

"Let me see," he replied. "If I remember my Bible stories . . ."

He paused, recalling the Old Testament history he had studied and read. "Jacob, the son of Isaac, the grandson of Abraham, had a dream after he stole his brother's birthright. It was a dream about a ladder stretching from earth to heaven, a ladder with angels going up and down it."

Rose remembered the story she had been told when she was a little girl and attended the Lutheran church down the road from where she lived. She went there to Vacation Bible School every summer. She learned all of the stories then.

"Esau," she said. "Esau was his twin brother, the older of the two."

"And Esau was the one who was supposed to get the blessing, but Jacob tricked both his brother and his father and got the blessing," Thomas added.

"But I never understood the dream," Rose said. "Why did he have a dream of angels ascending and descending near him when he had done something so reprehensible?" she asked. "Why would he receive this wonderful vision, a promise that he would have many children and would be able to return to his homeland? Why, when he had done something so horrible to his own family, would God promise Jacob that He would always be with him?"

Thomas considered the question. "Mercy, I guess." Then he explained what he meant. "It was a dream for which we are all desperate, the dream that promises restoration, the dream that says we will one day return to that joyful Garden of Eden, to completeness. And that even though we are exiled at the hand of someone we have wronged or if we wander far away on our own accord, we will always have the vehicle to get us home again, the ladder filled with angels bringing us back to the fold."

Rose pondered this. She suddenly remembered her

own dream as she'd lain upon the mystery ladder, the colors and the faraway cries, a place that harbored no such commodity. She recalled the way the dream had come to her, as if it had been the dream of someone else, as if it had been passed to her. She thought about the way she fell through darkness.

"Jacob's ladder," she said softly, still thinking about the connection between the Bible story and the one at hand. "But this story didn't turn out so good," she added. "This Jacob got murdered; he received no mercy."

"Well, maybe that's the purpose of an afterlife," Thomas replied. "Maybe the mercy we don't find here, we'll find there."

A barge moved along the river. They both glanced up to watch the vessel as it passed. It was long and empty except for a few old tires and large spools of rope. Lights danced along the sides. One man stood inside the small captain's cabin. They waited until it was all the way to the bridge before speaking again.

"Rip came by yesterday," Rose finally said, glad to be able to tell him about everything that had happened.

He nodded.

She saw that he had already heard. "Mary?" she guessed, remembering that her friend had also told the sheriff.

"Lou Ellen again," he replied. "She was in quite the confessional mode. She told me practically everything, about you, about her. Some of it was more than I really wanted to know." He smiled. "Anyway, she said that you were upset that he was here, that he brought his new wife with him."

Rose didn't reply.

"She said she didn't know what you talked about," Thomas said. "That you didn't tell her that."

Rose nodded. She remembered how she had felt after her ex-husband drove away, how she hadn't mentioned to her friends his reason for coming. She wondered if Thomas was waiting for her to tell him, whether he was curious about what had been exchanged between her and her ex-husband. But she understood that being nosy was not a trait of this man she had come to love. Thomas was content to wait to hear from her only when she was ready to tell. That was one of things that drew her to him, the ease with which he let her unfold her stories.

"It's my father," she said, not really having a reason to keep the news to herself any longer. Besides, she realized, she had already told Sheriff Montgomery. She might as well tell the person who mattered most to her, she decided. "Rip said that his condition has worsened and that I should go back to Rocky Mount to let him say his good-byes."

Thomas waited awhile before making a reply. Rose could tell by the way he hesitated that he was being very careful with the words he chose, that he understood the weight of the situation.

"And what do you think?" he finally asked,

knowing some of the history between Rose and her only surviving parent.

"I think I don't owe my father anything else. I think it was out of line for Rip to come here with his new bride and tell me this. I don't want to be told that I have to go back there. If I go home, I'll expect him to apologize for all that he put me through, and I'm afraid that once again I'll be gravely disappointed and that I'll be the one to come away feeling guilty." She drew in a breath. "I'm tired of thinking about him and having to sort through more emotions than a person should have to deal with in one lifetime." She looked away.

"Why didn't he tell my brother, who, by the way, lives less than ten miles from the nursing home? Why is it that I'm always the one who has to attend to him?"

Thomas didn't respond. He knew Rose's questions weren't really meant to be answered.

"When do you have to make your decision?" he asked.

"I don't know," she said with a sigh. "If he's as bad as Rip says, then I guess sometime soon."

Thomas nodded; then he cupped her chin in his hand and gently turned her head so that she was facing him.

"It doesn't matter to any of us what you choose," he said softly. "We all love you, Rose; Lou Ellen, Mary, Rhonda, Lucas, and I, and we always will."

He reached up and slid a piece of hair away from the wound on her forehead.

Rose thought he was going to say something more, but he didn't. She expected that he would tell her what he thought she should do, or say he'd go with her, or give her other alternatives to think about. But he only held her. He didn't say another thing until they walked to her camper and he kissed her good night, and then it was only the promise that he would see her in the morning. She watched him walk up the driveway and down the lane toward his place.

Later, however, when she slid into her bed, stretched, and then curled under the cover of a light blanket, she thought about his comment, and she understood completely. What Thomas had said and what he had not said were exactly right. And in spite of the harrowing events of her day, Rose fell fully and calmly into sleep.

TWENTY-TWO

It was late when Rose was finally roused from her sleep. She had slept long and deeply, but she did not feel rested when she woke. She felt troubled, exposed in the way she used to feel as a child and as a young married woman, the way she hadn't felt in months.

She tried to shake it off and glanced over at the clock on the microwave oven and saw that it was almost 11:00 A.M. She wondered why someone hadn't stopped by or called. She was usually at the office well before that late-morning hour and she was

199

surprised that Mary hadn't driven over in the golf cart or Thomas hadn't arrived at her door to wake her up for work or at least to check on her.

When she sat up, however, the thin skin stretched and swollen across her forehead, an ache instantly reminding her of her recent injury, she saw that she had left the shades on the window by her bed open. Anyone walking by could have seen that she was asleep.

She guessed that she had been looked in on and then left alone. Probably more than once, she thought, realizing how concerned Mary and Ms. Lou Ellen and Thomas had been the night before. She knew that it had been evident to everyone at the cabin that she was tired and in need of a little extra sleep.

She stood up from the bed, a bit wobbly, and fixed a pot of coffee. She wondered where the old and familiar feeling had been for so long, wondered why it had suddenly been brought to the surface once again—if it was a consequence of her headache or of the pending decision she knew she would have to make.

She found the milk in her refrigerator and set it out by the sink. Then she went into the bathroom, threw some water on her face, and looked at herself in the mirror. The wound on her forehead was now blue, the cut had healed over, and the swelling had diminished a bit. All that was left was a large bruise, a slender line above her brow, and the dull throbbing sensation that reminded her of how it felt to slam against the window of Sheriff Montgomery's car.

She studied the injury and decided a little foundation and powder would cover most of the discoloration. After she brushed her teeth and combed her hair, she reached for her makeup bag to disguise the wound and also add a little pink to her cheeks.

As she stared at herself in the mirror, the small sponge carefully blotting against her skin, she leaned in closer, her eyes and the bones of her jaw magnified, and suddenly noticed, to her great surprise, how much she looked like her father. In that instant of recognition, she understood the bump on her head had not been the source of her discontent.

As a child, Rose remembered, she had favored her mother. They shared the same peach skin, the thick dark hair, the faint glow of hopefulness. But this time, as she studied her reflection, recalling only glimpses of her mother from outdated photographs yellowed from time and wrinkled from constant folding and unfolding, and realizing that she had aged well past the early and untimely year of her mother's death, she peered at herself and recognized only her father returning the gaze. The wide nose, the thin brow, the dark nature of his large brown eyes, all of the features of the man she had hidden from most of her life, were now completely hers.

She watched him, pondered him, regarded him. And then she said out loud, as if he were in the room listening, as if he had told her what she had seen for herself, "There you are again."

Rose put down the sponge and went into the kitchen to get a cup of coffee. She sat down at her table, trying to erase the reflection from her mind, the trouble in her heart. She knew she would have to decide what to do about visiting her father soon enough, but she didn't want to be reminded of him first thing in the morning. She didn't want to see him so clearly, so closely, and she didn't want to be locked again in the grips of her family's dark history, her father's heavy hand.

She finished her coffee, dressed, and, without the aid of a mirror, continued putting on her makeup. She walked to the office, sorting through the memories, the possibilities, and the matters at hand.

It was cloudy, still cool for the late-morning hour. Rose walked up the driveway, noticing that the group heading to Texas was gone, that a new rig from California was parked three sites down from hers, a large motor home, the expensive kind, with three bedrooms and top-of-the-line appliances. She eyed the luxurious vehicle, the heavily shaded windows, wishing she could get a closer view, and wondered who was staying in such nice accommodations.

She walked beyond the line of sites on the river and headed past the area that was closed to campers, the yellow police tape still marking the entrance, barring people from heading down to the murder site. She stopped, looked over in the field to the empty place where the camper had been parked, and then moved to the office.

Mary and Ms. Lou Ellen were sitting at the desk behind the counter.

"Rose is finally up," Mary announced.

Both women turned to their friend as she walked in the door. Relief appeared to settle upon their faces. The dog sat up by the counter and wagged his tail.

"Darling Rose, how are you this morning?" Ms. Lou Ellen asked.

Rose went right to her and, without an answer, leaned over and kissed her friend on the top of her head. Ms. Lou Ellen reached up and took Rose by the hand. She held it for a few minutes.

The act was Rose's way of saying she was fine, of releasing her friend from the guilt that Thomas had said she suffered, and of signaling her affection for the woman who had become so important to her. She wanted her to know not only that was she forgiven but that she was greatly admired and loved. She stood up and smiled, stepping a few feet away from the table.

"I am fit as a fiddle," she finally replied, not revealing the fretful way she had slept, the decision with which she wrestled, the old veil of trouble now pressing down hard upon her.

"Your head look better," Mary responded.

She had stood up from her desk and walked over, examining the wound they remembered from the previous night. Mary had already been by her camper at least three times that morning. She had observed her friend's chest rise and fall, saw her body change positions on her bed, and, confident that she was alive and breathing, had decided not to wake her.

"It feels better today," Rose replied with a smile. "I think being back in my own little camper helped tremendously."

Ms. Lou Ellen nodded with a wink. "Did you sleep, dear, or did Thomas fulfill his duty?"

She slid papers off of the chair beside her, making room for Rose to sit down.

" 'Fulfill his duty'?" Rose asked, surprised by the question, uncertain of the meaning behind it.

The older woman smiled. "Keeping you awake?"

Rose sat down.

"He was supposed to make sure you didn't go right to sleep," she said. Then she pointed to her own temple as further means of explanation. "Because of your head wound, dear." She appeared puzzled at Rose's reaction.

"Oh," Rose responded. "His duty . . . I was thinking . . . Well, never mind what I was thinking."

Rose rested her elbows on the table. "We stayed up a little while, but I had been alert and conscious for at least six hours since the injury. That's enough time to allow for concussion-related problems."

"I see," the older woman replied. "Well, you are the nurse." She smiled.

"So, what have I missed this morning?" Rose asked.

She reached down and petted the dog. "Lester Earl, you seem to have made a home for yourself here."

The dog stood up and then headed to where Mary had returned. He curled himself between her legs.

"He's trying to win Mary's heart," Ms. Lou Ellen reported, watching the dog.

"He's your husband," Mary snapped. She spun around, whipping her legs past the dog, who yelped and then hobbled over to the older woman.

"Ex-husband, Mary dear," Ms. Lou Ellen replied. "He has his freedom to charm any woman he chooses. And it appears as if he has chosen you."

"It's okay, Lester Earl," Rose said as she turned around and faced the counter where Mary was standing. "It takes her awhile, but she'll warm up to you. She did with me when I showed up unattended." She turned back around, reached across the table, and took part of the newspaper her friend was reading.

"Yes, but I warm up to you because you give me lunch break," Mary said, eyeing Ms. Lou Ellen's companion.

Rose thought she saw a hint of a smile coming from her friend. She did not comment.

"That's the only reason?" she asked.

"Of course," Mary replied.

"Well, I never thought I'd see such a thing. Mary demonstrating good humor." Ms. Lou Ellen grinned.

Mary made a hissing noise, moved to her seat at the desk, and began reading the mail.

"So, what's happening in West Memphis today?" Rose asked. She skimmed over the front page.

"Just the usual," Ms. Lou Ellen replied. "A couple

of car wrecks, at least one church supper, and high school baseball." She was reading the obituaries.

Rose flipped through the section she had picked up, wondering if there had been any mention of her kidnapping or of the murder of the man from New Mexico.

"Clyde Gilbert died," the older woman said somberly. "He had cancer, I think. And he was a very sweaty man, if I remember correctly."

"Well, I assume it was the cancer that killed him, since I don't recall ever hearing of death by perspiration," Rose responded.

"Doesn't say," she replied. "The family will receive guests later this evening."

"Maybe you take them some of Rose's funeral food," Mary suggested as she threw away some junk mail.

"That's a lovely idea, Mary dear." Ms. Lou Ellen immediately placed the paper on the desk. She appeared excited. "I think I'll go right over and see what I have that's ideal for that family."

She stood up from her seat and walked over to the counter. "Would you say chicken casserole or beef stew?" she asked her friends.

"Hmmm," Rose replied. She appeared deep in thought regarding this question. "I think it goes back to what you remember about his condition, that it would matter whether he died from the cancer or from the sweat," she said, attempting to be humorous.

"I see your point exactly," Ms. Lou Ellen replied

seriously. "A long-term illness speaks more of a stew or beef-based entrée."

Mary and Rose faced each other. They were both surprised by their friend's thoughts.

"And a sudden death is more of a poultry-themed meal." She tapped her finger on the counter in deep consideration.

"Stew," Rose said. "I'd definitely go with the stew."

The older woman turned to Mary for confirmation, but the office manager only shrugged her shoulders.

"Yes?" Ms. Lou Ellen asked, and grinned, "Then beef stew it is. Thank you so much for your assistance." She nodded in Rose's direction.

"Lester, would you like to return home with me, or would you prefer to stay with these two comely women?"

The dog looked at Rose and then at Mary, who sneered at him, and immediately bolted for the door. Ms. Lou Ellen raised her brows and nodded, as if she understood the dog's decision.

"Drop by and see me, Rose," the older woman said as she headed out. "I really must hear more about your incident." She waved and walked outside, moving toward her cabin.

"You shouldn't be so hard on the dog," Rose said as she put down the paper and eyed the coffeepot. She could tell there was still some left from the morning brew. She poured herself a cup and sat down in the seat Ms. Lou Ellen had previously occupied. She was now across from her friend. Mary waved away the comment.

"Any new campers?" she asked Mary.

"Two," the manager reported. "One on number forty-five, the other near you, number seventy-eight," she added.

Rose knew she meant the expensive rig she had recently seen that was just around the drive from her casita. Number seventy-eight was a nice site, a large pull-through near the bathhouse and the laundry room. "Family or single?" she asked.

"Don't know," Mary said. "They check in late." She reached up for the registration book. "California," she said, searching for and locating the card. "Can't read the name."

"Family from South Carolina at number forty-five. They arrived yesterday, staying two nights." she explained.

Rose nodded. She continued to skim across the paper, not finding any story about what had happened to her. She did find a small report on the inside front page about the murder at Shady Grove Campground still being investigated. It said that there were no new details and that the name of the deceased was still being withheld while family members were being notified.

Rose remembered the two men she had met the day before, the nephew and his son, John and Daniel Sunspeaker. She remembered the slow and careful way they'd acted toward her, the kindness of the older man as he gave her the dressing for her wound.

She wondered if the sheriff had seen the two of

them that morning, if the camper had arrived safely at the sheriff's office, and if the family members knew about the ladder. She decided that she should go to town and find out what she could. She noticed the clock. She knew Mary would need her lunch break first.

"You hungry?" she asked.

Mary nodded. "Maybe I just go next door and get some funeral stew," she said.

Rose smiled. "Sounds like a good idea to me." Then she put down the paper and moved over to the desk to see what work needed to be done. When she noticed the message book, she remembered something.

"By the way, did that FBI agent ever come by here yesterday, the one who called?" she asked.

She remembered her conversation with the sheriff and that he claimed he didn't know anything about the Federal Bureau of Investigation being involved in the case. She assumed the man never showed.

Mary nodded, and the affirmative answer surprised Rose. "He came about ten o'clock," she replied. "When he found out the camper had been stolen, he left very quickly." She closed the registration book and straightened the papers on her desk. "He was very upset," she added.

"Did he show you a badge?" Rose asked, thinking that this man, like the one pretending to be a Highway Patrol officer, might have been impersonating an agent.

"No," Mary said. "Just told me his name and where

he was from." She finished cleaning up her desk and prepared to leave for lunch. "I remembered the phone call."

"And where was he from?" Rose asked as she sat down.

"Louisiana," Mary replied.

Rose waited. The name of the state startled her, though she didn't know why.

"Natchez," Mary added, and Rose turned quickly to her.

"Good-looking tall man, long hair, from Natchez, Louisiana."

Rose immediately remembered the stranger she had seen in town at the sheriff's office and at the library. She fell back against the seat at the desk and a long, cold shiver ran down the entire length of her spine.

TWENTY-THREE

After Mary returned from her lunch break, Rose gave the manager the few messages she had taken, then headed out of the office to her car, which was parked at her campsite. She had decided that she was going into town to find the sheriff and get permission to search inside the camper again. She also wanted to speak to the family members of the dead man to see if they knew anything about the secret compartment and the ladder that was hidden inside his travel trailer.

Rose considered paying Ms. Lou Ellen a visit first, but when she peeked in the window at the cabin, she saw that her friend had already left. She assumed she had picked out the perfect grief dish and was on her way to deliver it. She saw the dog curled up by the door, and for the first time, she wondered if the dead man's family would want the dog returned. She wasn't sure how her friend would feel about having to give him up. She decided that choice would not be hers to make and that she would let Ms. Lou Ellen handle that situation when the time came.

She walked along the entryway and rounded the corner of the drive, moving very fast. She traveled that path so many times every day, she'd quit paying attention to her direction anymore. She usually stared at the river or over toward Thomas's place.

As with previous trips, she wasn't watching where she was heading, and before she knew what had happened, Rose ran right into the owner of the California motor home. He was outside fiddling with something in the front of his vehicle.

"Whoa there, missy," the man said, catching Rose before she knocked them both down.

"My goodness, I am sorry," Rose insisted. She stepped back, embarrassed at what had happened. "Are you okay?" she asked.

She touched her head, remembering the recent injury. She was glad not to have caused herself more harm.

"I'm fine," the man replied. "But it looks like you

might need to be more careful." He seemed to notice the bump and the bruise.

Rose studied the man. He was stocky, broad across the chest, and had wide shoulders. He was fifty or sixty—Rose couldn't tell precisely—and he appeared to be a man of money. He was wearing a beige silk shirt with narrow brown thread delicately sewn along the seams and borders, tan linen pants, and soft leather designer shoes, as well as a belt made of the same tawny color. The large belt buckle was carved from a thick, heavy piece of blue-green turquoise. He had on a silver chain that dropped beneath his collar, and his hair was black and slicked down, giving it a wet appearance.

Rose thought he looked nothing like a man who traveled by camper, even a camper as nice as the one he stood in front of, and when she remembered what he drove, she turned to get a better view of it.

"I just got this thing," the man said, noticing her interest in his rig. "I'm not sure I know how to get it all connected properly," he added. "I figured out the electricity and the water last night when I arrived, but this"—he picked up the long plastic pipe that he had dropped when she ran into him—"I don't know where this goes."

Rose could see that he was trying to hook up his sewer line. He appeared completely helpless. She was in a hurry, but, remembering her job at Shady Grove and her duty to aid the other campers, she delayed her departure to assist him.

"Here," she said, taking the connector from him. She walked around to the side where the appropriate attachment was located, knelt down, removed the cap, and fit one end of the black plastic pipe to it. Then she moved to the side of the vehicle and reattached it to the opening underneath. "Just make certain both ends are secure," she said, reaching up and making sure it was a tight fit. "And you'll probably want to get a support attachment to put underneath it," she added, standing and wiping her hands on her legs, "if you plan to camp a lot."

"A support attachment?" the man asked, clearly displaying his ignorance. They moved toward the front of the vehicle.

"It's a long piece of plastic with small grooved legs. It just keeps your line off the ground, gives it a little gravity. Then you won't get so filthy hooking and unhooking."

She noticed his clothes and thought of saying something about dressing more casually for camper maintenance, then decided against it.

"Every rig is different, but the valve to turn it on and off should be somewhere near the cap." She could tell by the expression on his face that he would never find it, so she returned to the hookup site, knelt back down, reached underneath, and twisted the valve.

She stood up and headed toward him again. "It's open now, should work okay." Then she asked, "Is this your first time camping?"

He smiled at her, stuck out his hand. "Robert Wellington," he said, introducing himself. "From Stockton, California," he added. "And yes, this would be my first time in a campground."

Rose grinned. She held up her hands reminding him that she had just handled his sewer line.

He nodded, understanding.

Rose thought the man was attractive, charming, even if he was clueless about camping.

"Rose Franklin," she said. "I live here, three sites down." She pointed with her chin in the direction of her camper. "It takes a little while to figure things out, but once you do, it's simple after that."

He smiled and turned to see her rig, then turned back around to face her. "Pretty here," he said. "The river and all." He looked across the Mississippi. "I could see why you might stay here." He peered at Rose.

She nodded in agreement. "What brought you to West Memphis?" she asked, stepping away from the rig and closer to the driveway.

"I'm an art dealer," he replied. "I'm here to see about some pieces."

Rose turned her face toward the town across the river. "In Memphis?" she asked, thinking it would make more sense that his pieces would be there rather than in Arkansas. She knew there wasn't much in the way of art on her side of the Mississippi.

He shook his head. "No," he replied. "Here in West Memphis."

Rose was surprised.

"Well, where are my manners?" he said as he moved over to the door of his vehicle. "Please, come in and wash your hands."

He demonstrated a bit of difficulty opening the door. Rose smiled and walked over, sliding open the latch.

He stepped aside. "Maybe you could give me a few lessons about motor homes," he said, pulling the door open and gesturing for her to go in.

Rose walked up the steps. She knew she should be getting to town, but she was interested in seeing the interior of the large vehicle, a class-A motor home. She had been in only one since staying at Shady Grove, and that wasn't as big as this one. She moved inside the entryway. Mr. Wellington came in behind her.

It was beautiful and had leather furniture, stainless-steel appliances, and thick woven rugs. Rose had never seen such luxury in a motor home before. She couldn't help the sounds of delight she was making as she glanced around, taking everything in.

She turned to her right and saw the driver's quarters, an oversized cab with room for three or four people to sit comfortably. Then she peered down the hallway on her left and saw two closed doors, which she assumed led to the bedrooms. And then, remaining where she was standing in the entryway, she spotted something else. "You've even got a fireplace!" she exclaimed.

Mr. Wellington appeared amused that his guest was so taken by the motor home he had only recently purchased. "Here, please," he said, inviting her to see the entire unit.

Rose shook her head in amazement. She slowly walked through the living room, past the kitchen, stopping to admire the fireplace with gas logs, and then headed into the master bedroom. That room alone was almost twice the size of her entire trailer. She was impressed.

"Well, this is hardly what I call camping," she said, returning to where he stood, still taking in everything around her. She tried not to touch anything, but she certainly felt the temptation. She remembered her hands, and, recognizing her concern, he pointed her to the sink in the bathroom behind the master suite.

Rose turned around, walked in the direction from which she had just come, and entered the plush bathroom. She headed over to the sink and washed her hands. She eyed the marble shower and the heavy Italian tile carefully placed on the floor, the golden fixtures, and the white porcelain sink. Then she regarded the beveled glass and the large skylight above her head.

After washing with a fragrant lavender soap, she searched around for a towel and saw a small closet near the toilet. Thinking that it might have the linen inside, she opened the door and saw shelves of heavy cotton towels and stacks of neatly pressed sheets. On the floor was a cardboard box that appeared completely out of place with all of the other luxurious items. She took one of the small hand towels and stared into the box.

Curiosity getting the best of her, she flipped open the lid and saw three pots. They were all large and differently shaped. Each bore markings, intricate patterns along the sides. They reminded her of the petroglyphs she had been studying, and she knew immediately that they were Indian pots.

She quickly closed the lid and placed the used towel beside the sink. She checked her reflection in the mirror and headed to the kitchen, where Mr. Wellington was making drinks.

"Soda?" he asked as he put ice in two glasses.

"Sure," she replied, stepping around to the living room and standing by the sofa. She watched as he poured some soda from a bottle into the glasses and then walked over to her, handing her one.

"This is quite a motor home," Rose said, taking a sip. "It's unbelievable really."

The man smiled. "Well, it's as close to home away from home as I could find." He motioned her over to sit down. She complied.

"Yeah, well it's better than any home I ever had," she said, remembering the houses in which she had lived.

She glanced around the walls and noticed a few paintings, a wall hanging.

"It's Navajo," he said, noticing her interest in the short, narrow piece that hung next to the window.

"Lovely," she responded. She liked the rich colors, the delicate, smooth weaving pattern, the intricate design of the thick cotton threads.

"You must like Indian art," she observed, thinking about the pots she had seen, as well as his belt buckle and the wall hanging.

"I admire all art, but yes, I particularly appreciate the art of this country's native people," he said, taking a sip of his drink.

She nodded.

"Every piece tells a story, and I find I like collecting the stories of others." He bore a look of pride.

Rose finished her drink, suddenly recalling her task of finding the ladder, and knew she needed to get into town. She wanted to talk to Sheriff Montgomery and examine once again the dead man's camper before the family drove it away. She stood up from the sofa.

"Well, good luck to you, Mr. Wellington. Let me know if you have any more trouble getting hooked up." She walked into the kitchen and placed her glass in the sink. He followed her with his eyes.

"I work at the office and I've been camping awhile. I can answer most questions. Or if I can't, I can certainly find someone who can."

She glanced out of the window and suddenly noticed that there was no other vehicle for the man to drive. She wondered how he planned to conduct his business.

"You have transportation into town?" she asked, turning around to face him.

He nodded. "I have friends here," he replied. "They'll be along soon enough to drive me to where I plan to conduct my business."

"Great," Rose responded, holding out her hand to shake his. "I guess I'll see you around."

He set down his glass, stood up from his seat, and shook her hand. Then he walked to the front door and opened it, this time taking note as to where the latch was located.

"Yes," he said. "I imagine you will."

Rose exited the motor home, hurried inside her own camper, found her keys, and got into her car.

She waved as she passed the man she had just met and immediately noticed in her rearview mirror that he was watching her even as she drove away from the campsites and headed past the office.

"Interesting guy," she said to herself as she left Shady Grove. "But I hope he can get his money back on the motor home, because he'll never make it camping." She laughed to herself as she made the turn into town.

TWENTY-FOUR

By the time Rose arrived at the sheriff's office, it was mid-afternoon. She parked and walked up to the front door, noticing that most of the staff seemed to have left for the day. When she got inside, she didn't find one of the familiar receptionists. She stood at the front desk and then peeked around the corner into the large room with cubicles. She didn't see a soul.

"Hello?" she called out, surprised to find the doors unlocked and nobody inside. "Anybody home?"

There was no reply.

"Hello?" she yelled again.

"Yeah, just a minute," a voice responded.

Rose heard a toilet flush and a door close. She had obviously interrupted someone.

Rose waited, feeling a bit embarrassed by her intrusion. She noticed the clock on the wall. It was after 3:00 P.M. It surprised her to find so much of the day had gone. She looked out in the parking lot and saw that the sheriff's car was not there. She remembered the accident from the day before and assumed the front end was being repaired.

"Oh, hello again." It was the same deputy who had taken her statement the first day of the murder investigation. He was tucking in his shirt.

She had forgotten his name, but he recognized her. "Ms. Franklin," he said.

"Hey," Rose replied cheerfully. "Good to see you again."

He smiled. "Roy," he remarked. It appeared he could tell she didn't remember him by name. "Everybody's gone," he reported.

"I see," she replied. "Guess it's getting late."

"Well, it's almost quitting time anyway," he explained. He smoothed down the sides of his hair.

"So, what can I help you with?" he asked. "Think of something else to add to your statement?"

He eyed her, noticed the bruise on her forehead, and remembered hearing about her reported kidnapping, the trip the sheriff had to make to Oklahoma to pick her up and bring her home. "Or are you here to make another one?" He grinned.

"No, I've made all the statements I'm required to, Roy," she replied, adding his name just to sound smart.

He examined her closely. "Maybe up until now, but from what I hear, we might ought to keep out a running statement for you." He leaned against the doorframe, waiting for her response. Apparently, he thought he was being funny.

"Yeah, whatever," she replied, deciding not to engage in this conversation.

"I was trying to find the sheriff," she said. "Is he in?"

The deputy stared at her for a minute, disappointed that she wouldn't play along.

"Nah." He shook his head and stood up straight. "He's been gone most of the day. Had to take the car over to the body shop this morning; then he had to meet with somebody about the murder. He was supposed to be back by now. He missed lunch."

Rose waited for him to continue. It sounded to her like there was more he was going to say. There was.

"It was a retirement party for one of the girls," he said. "We met at Marco's at twelve o'clock. Montgomery was supposed to be the master of cere-monies." The deputy stretched his back and twisted from side to side, as if he was tired of sitting.

"That doesn't sound like the sheriff," Rose said, surprised at this news. "Has anybody heard from him?" she asked.

"Yeah, he called about eleven-thirty and said to go on without him, that he would try to get there as soon as he could. Then he said to make up for it, everybody could go home a couple of hours early." He nodded. "So everybody did."

"But you," Rose said, stating the obvious.

"Right. I wanted to finish some of my desk work."

That explains where everyone is, Rose thought. "Did he say who he was meeting?" Rose asked.

The deputy narrowed his eyes at the woman. He wasn't sure how much he should reveal. Rose could tell he was sizing her up.

"I just want to speak to him about something I remembered from the crime scene." She thought that would make him feel better about her reason to see his boss.

He nodded. "He said some government agent had contacted him. I guess that means the FBI. Anyway, he said that he was going to meet him at his house, escort him over to the impound lot, and introduce him to the victim's family."

Rose didn't know what lot he meant.

Seeing her puzzlement, he explained. "The impound lot," he repeated. "Down on Second Street, by the warehouses," he added. "Where we keep the vehicles we take."

"Oh," Rose responded. Then she thought for a minute. "The camper, is that where that is?" she asked.

"I guess," he replied. "I haven't heard from Bunker—he's the one who brought it back. But it doesn't matter, because you can't go in there." He folded his arms across his chest, a gesture of authority that she recognized as one of many her father used to give.

"I didn't say I was planning to go in there," she replied. She was growing impatient with the deputy's attitude. She tried to keep her cool.

"Well, from what I hear, that'll be the first time you do what you're supposed to do." He stared at her.

Rose chose not to respond to his wisecrack. "May I use the phone?" she asked, pointing to the main phone on the front desk. She figured if she couldn't see the sheriff, she might as well try to contact the dead man's relatives.

"Be my guest," he replied. "Just close the door behind you when you leave. I'm going back to finish my paperwork," he added. Then he turned and headed toward the row of desks.

Rose picked up the receiver and dialed information. She asked for the number for the Motel 8 off of I-40, the place they had dropped off the victim's nephew and his son. The hotel clerk answered the phone.

"John Sunspeaker's room," Rose requested.

The operator paused. Rose assumed she was locating the room number.

"I can ring it for you," the clerk replied. "But I saw them leave not more than an hour ago, and they haven't come back."

"Oh." Rose wasn't sure whether or not to leave a message. The Sunspeakers might not remember her, and she didn't know if they would even want to see anyone after identifying the body and making all the arrangements they would have to make.

"They left with the police," the clerk reported, sounding eager to share the news. "But I don't think they were in trouble or anything," she added.

Rose could only guess about the gossip exchanged at interstate motels.

"Was it the sheriff?" Rose asked.

"You mean Montgomery?" the clerk replied.

"Yeah." At first, it surprised Rose to hear his name, but then she realized that probably everybody in West Memphis knew who the sheriff was.

"Nah, I ain't seen him," she said. "This was a guy dressed in a dark uniform."

Rose could hear her talking to another guest. She waited a minute. "What kind of dark uniform?" she then asked, startled that another law officer would have been sent to pick the Sunspeakers up. The people at the sheriff's departments wore light-colored uniforms, a tan shirt and pants.

"I don't know." The clerk hesitated. "Can you hold on a minute?"

"Sure," Rose said.

She listened to the clerk doing a transaction with another guest. There was a little chatter. The minutes passed.

"There. Sorry," the clerk announced. "Who were you waiting for?" she asked, having forgotten the conversation she had been having with Rose.

"The Sunspeakers," Rose said. "You were saying they left with a uniformed officer."

"Oh yeah, that's right."

"Do you remember what kind of uniform it was?" Rose asked.

The woman paused again. "It was dark, looked like a patrolman's uniform."

"Highway Patrol?" Rose asked.

"Yeah," she answered. "But not from Arkansas, I know some of those guys." She started another conversation with somebody else in the office.

"Where, then?" Rose asked, trying to get her attention.

"What?" the clerk replied.

"Where was the patrolman from?" she asked, her voice slightly raised.

"From Oklahoma," the clerk reported, sounding weary of the conversation. "Look, I got to go."

"Wait," Rose shouted, hoping she hadn't hung up yet. "Did he say his name?"

"What?"

"Did the patrolman give his name?" Rose dreaded the answer.

"Yeah, I think it was"—she paused—"Cupwell. Or maybe Capwell? I'm not sure."

"Caldwell?" Rose almost shouted.

"That's it, Caldwell." The woman seemed pleased with herself. "So, do you want to leave a message?"

Rose threw down the phone without a reply.

"Deputy!" She called out as she hurried around the front desk. "Deputy, we got trouble!"

"What's the matter with you?" he asked as he stood up and slowly made his way from his desk to where Rose was standing.

"This FBI agent that the sheriff was supposed to meet—did he mention his name?" Rose asked.

She assumed that there was a connection between the sheriff's long absence and the two men being escorted away by the impersonating officer.

The deputy seemed to be thinking. Rose couldn't wait.

"This is important," she said. "Did he say his name was Caldwell?"

The deputy noticed her agitated state and thought again for a minute, "No," he replied. "I don't remember him saying his name. He just said where he was from."

Rose's face instantly lost all its color. "Where was that?" she asked. "Where was the agent from?"

"Natchez, I think," the deputy replied, not following the woman's line of questioning or her sudden concern. "Somewhere from over in Louisiana," he added.

Rose ran to the door, stopped, and turned to the deputy.

"Call for backup, and go to the impound lot. See if they're there. I'll go to Sheriff Montgomery's house first. Hurry! And be careful," she added. "The sheriff is in danger!"

Rose ran to her car and jumped in, not waiting for a response from the deputy. She didn't know what she might find at Sheriff Montgomery's house or even if she should go alone. She only hoped that she wasn't too late.

TWENTY-FIVE

Rose remembered where the sheriff lived because she had visited him during the holidays. The entire gang from Shady Grove—Lucas, Rhonda, Ms. Lou Ellen, Mary, Thomas, and Rose—had driven together to the farm near the edge of town for his annual West Memphis Christmas party. Rose had heard it was the town event of the year, and once they arrived, she realized that assessment was true.

Sheriff Montgomery had hay rides for the children on sleighs pulled by horses. There were two bonfires down near the finger of the Mississippi River, which marked the edge of his property. There was a pig roast, tubs of coleslaw, eggnog, and more than a dozen desserts.

They had a bluegrass band playing music, and the

high school chorus sang carols. He even had gifts for everyone when they departed. It seemed to Rose the entire town was invited to his party, and it was one of her favorite memories since arriving in West Memphis.

She sped down the main road and then exited onto the gravel one that led down to the sheriff's farm. She hoped that no one was there, that no trouble had yet occurred, and that the deputy would find everybody at the city lot before anyone was hurt.

She glanced around the wooded property as she drove down toward it. She checked out all of the places where people could be hiding and tried to convince herself that everything was going to be fine. She held to that thought as she continued down the driveway. She saw the house and immediately noticed that there were no cars in front. She let out a deep breath, then decided to make a quick turn around beside the house and return to the impound lot on Second Street.

Just as she whipped around the corner, she immediately came upon the dead man's camper parked just behind the house. It surprised her and she wondered how it had gotten there and who was with it. She stopped the car, waited for signs of somebody, saw nothing, and finally got out and searched around.

Rose tried to guess how many people might be on the property, if Caldwell and the agent were the only bad guys involved. She wondered if they had already found what they were looking for and had left the sheriff and the two family members somewhere near the house. She tried not to think about what condition they might be in.

She crept around the vehicle and the house, hearing nothing, seeing no one. She was about to go into the house, check the inside, and then place a call to the deputy, when she suddenly heard voices from out near the riverbank.

She listened, and the conversation sounded as if it was coming from the lane beside the house and then she heard noises down by the barn. It seemed as if there were people either in the small wooded area in front of the water or all the way down at the river. She headed cautiously in that direction.

She sneaked down the lane, easing into the barn. She decided to search for a weapon, since she didn't have anything to protect herself. She looked around, finding only fishing poles and brooms. Finally, she saw the handle of an ax. She picked it up, thinking it would at least be something to swing, and then she slipped into the woods.

Moving from tree to tree, she heard two voices. She recognized only one, the sheriff's, although the other one sounded vaguely familiar.

As she edged her way toward the river, she peeked from behind a scrub oak and saw a man. He was holding up a ladder, a beautiful, rugged stone-laden ladder. She guessed that it was the ladder Caldwell had wanted, the one she had fallen upon in Mr. Sunspeaker's camper. She studied the man holding the ladder and recognized him immediately as the tall, dark stranger she had encountered twice before.

He was no FBI agent, she knew, and once she saw his big rugged hands, she guessed that he was the strangler and that he must have tied up the sheriff or captured him in some manner. She figured that the lawman was somewhere close by, since she could still make out his voice, though not his words.

Without knowing what else to do, she charged from the woods and, relying completely upon the element of surprise, knocked the man down with one swift, hard swing of the ax handle, right across his shoulders. He fell like an old tree.

"Rose!" the sheriff called out, running up from the river, throwing down a handful of plants. "What on earth have you done?"

She was surprised to see the sheriff completely unharmed and apparently gardening. She was startled that he appeared totally fine and obviously in no danger.

He hurried to the man and knelt down beside him, rolling him over. The man began to cough and sputter.

"The ladder?" he asked, stammering to talk. "Did I break the ladder?"

The sheriff glanced down beside the injured man and examined the object he had been holding. He shook his head.

"It's fine," he said, "but I'm not so sure I can say the same thing about you."

"What did you hit him with, Rose?" he asked,

trying to pull the man up to a sitting position.

Rose was confused. She still held the ax handle above her head.

"Put that down!" the sheriff commanded when he spotted her stance. "What are you thinking?" he asked.

The stranger sat up. He reached behind him and felt his shoulder blades. He coughed a few more times.

"I . . . I thought you were being held captive by the killer," she said, lowering the weapon she had used. "I came to help."

"Well, you helped Mr. Lujan right into a serious backache," the sheriff said, reaching down to feel the man's spine. "I don't think she broke anything."

The man bent forward a bit and grimaced.

"I'm still waiting for the justification for this unwarranted attack," the sheriff said heatedly.

"He's not FBI," Rose said, explaining. She recognized the name Lujan as the one Mary was trying to pronounce when she told about the phone call to Shady Grove.

"I know he's not FBI," the sheriff responded, kneeling beside the man, holding him across the shoulders.

"Then why has he been telling people he's FBI?" she asked.

"BIA," the man said, sounding short of breath.

"What?" Rose asked.

"Bureau of Indian Affairs," the sheriff said. "He's Philip Lujan, an agent of the Bureau of Indian Affairs."

"Oh," Rose said timidly.

"Now, do you want to tell me what on earth is going on?" the sheriff asked Rose. "Here, help me get him up."

She moved closer to the man and helped the sheriff pull him to his feet. He stood and then stumbled a few steps, leaned his hands on his knees, and took a few deep breaths. Sheriff Montgomery hurried over to the bank and brought up a plastic chair that he kept by the river for fishing.

"I told you I saw him in your office the day I gave my statement." Rose helped get the man in the chair. She lifted his shirt and saw the large red mark that was starting to swell. She had hit him pretty hard.

"I don't remember that," the sheriff said.

"Do you have any ice?" she asked.

"Yeah, but it's all the way at the house," he replied. "Philip, can you walk that far?"

"Give me a minute," the man responded.

"Keep talking, Rose," the lawman said to her as they stood beside the seated man.

"Well, I saw him next at the library and then I heard that an agent had called Mary at the campground, said he had talked to you, only you told me that you had not spoken to an agent," she explained.

"An FBI agent," he said. "You asked me about an FBI agent?" He shook his head, slid a hand through his hair.

Rose began to think through the mix-up, the fact that Mary, just like the deputy she had just spoken with, had simply guessed that Bureau meant the Federal Bureau of Investigation and that she was the one who had initially called Lujan a FBI agent.

"I came to find you because you didn't show up for work this afternoon," she continued.

"I called Roy and said I would be in later," he said.

"Yes, but—" Rose wasn't able to finish her statement. She'd intended to say Roy had told her about the call but that everyone still thought the sheriff would show up sometime.

"And then Philip and I got to talking," he continued, despite Rose's brief interruption. "And he explained why he was here and how the deceased had contacted him. The officer brought the camper to my house last night because he didn't have the keys to the impound lot. So, after I met Philip in town, we came home and searched it. And we found the ladder." He checked on Mr. Lujan again.

The man nodded his head to say he was feeling better.

"Well, why are you down at the river?" she asked.

"Because I grow yaupon here," he replied, remembering the holly plants he had dropped when he ran up.

"What's that?" she asked.

"Not that it's any of your business," he said, walking over to pick up the strewn pieces. "It's what the Indians used to brew to make a white drink, a tea," he explained. "I was giving a few of my plants to Agent Lujan."

She nodded as if she understood, even though she didn't, and then she bent down to check the man's wound. "I think I need to go get him some ice," she said, recognizing that would certainly help with the swelling that was starting.

Suddenly, Rose remembered the real imposter, Patrolman Caldwell, and the fact that he had taken the victim's family members hostage. She knew she had to tell the sheriff about that. However, just as she remembered what had led her there to his house, all three of them heard a car door slam. She and the sheriff immediately looked up in the direction of the barn.

Before she could warn the sheriff or the man from the Bureau of Indian Affairs, three men with guns walked out of the woods. John and Daniel Sunspeaker had their hands tied and were slowly being led out front.

TWENTY-SIX

What the—" the sheriff began.

Mr. Lujan tried to turn around to see what was happening behind him. He groaned, unable to twist himself while seated in the chair.

"Hello, Sheriff," the man pretending to be the Highway Patrol officer said. He had his gun pointed in the lawman's direction. "Let's get those hands up, shall we?"

He walked down to where Rose, Sheriff Montgomery, and Agent Lujan were gathered.

The other two guys had their guns on the men from New Mexico. Rose could see right away that the Sunspeakers were very frightened, but it appeared as if they had not been harmed.

Rose and the sheriff raised their hands. Caldwell glanced over at Rose.

"And so we meet again, Ms. Franklin," he said, moving to stand beside them. "How is it that you keep showing up everywhere I'm searching for something?" Then he turned around to get a better look at who was in the chair.

"What's the matter with you?" he asked. It was easy to see the man was in pain.

"I'm fine," Agent Lujan replied, choosing not to call attention to his injuries. "Just a cramp."

The man studied the agent.

"You're Lujan," he said. "I remember you from Natchez," he added. "And of course," he said, noticing the ladder on the ground beside him, "you came for the same thing we did." He grinned. "How kind of you to have this out for us," he said in a mocking tone. "It makes the rest of our time together so much easier."

Caldwell, dressed in a uniform, reached inside his pocket, took out a glove, and placed it on his left hand. Then he picked up the ladder, still closely watching those he had cornered. The gun was still in his hand.

No one moved.

"Where's your boss?" Agent Lujan asked, apparently familiar with the criminal.

Rose and Sheriff Montgomery faced each other. They were surprised that the two men were acquainted.

"I'm right where a good boss should be, behind the goons," a voice said, and a man emerged from the woods.

Rose turned to see the newest arrival at Shady Grove, Robert Wellington, moving in their direction. She shook her head and whispered to herself, "I should have known."

He walked right over to Rose, who still had her hands up in the air. He slid his thumb beneath her chin. She jerked away.

"Hello, neighbor," he said with a great deal of amusement in his voice. "I told Caldwell when he phoned me from Oklahoma to say you were in the camper that I could count on you to get me what I wanted." He winked. "And of course I was right."

Caldwell was holding the ladder. Wellington smiled when he saw the item and then faced Rose. "I recognized right away that you had a good eye for collectibles."

She did not respond.

"So you're the one who was harassing Sunspeaker. You're the one who murdered him," Lujan said, remaining in his seat.

"Well, well, well, Agent Lujan, you know the kind

of businessman I am." He walked over to the man sitting in the plastic chair.

"I know that you're in the business of stealing Indian artifacts, that you're in the illegal trade of sacred pieces," Lujan said.

The agent tried to stand up, but he was immediately pushed down by Caldwell, who was standing nearby.

"Now, you should know that I try to conduct my business on the up-and-up to begin with," Wellington explained. "The old man wouldn't bargain. I offered him a fair price. He wouldn't do business with me." There was a cold, eerie calm to his voice. "We always try to work things out before we resort to other means," he said, smiling at the agent. "This was just one of those times when things didn't go as smoothly as we had hoped."

It was clear that he didn't have a gun and that he was completely relying upon the others for the dirty work. They did not appear as if they were planning to let him down. They remained standing, pointing their firearms at Rose and the others.

Wellington went over to Caldwell and took the ladder from him. He held it up and examined it.

"You have to admit it's a spectacular piece," the man reported, nodding. "And of course, we can agree that I am very picky about what I collect."

"It's not yours to collect," John Sunspeaker called out suddenly.

His voice and his comment startled everyone. "It belongs to our people."

237

"Your people?" Wellington replied. "Your people are in New Mexico and have nothing to do with this ladder." He studied the stones. "You're Zuni."

"The first keeper of the ladder came from the east to *my people*. He put the pieces together, only to have it stolen later by *your people*. For more than three generations, we have searched for this ladder. It was my mother's brother who was given the dream to fulfill the promise of our ancestor. He was the one who recovered it and the one who replaced every missing stone. It became his responsibility to make sure it was returned to the tribe where it belongs." The dead man's nephew was flushed and visibly upset.

"Your mother's brother was a bad businessman," Wellington responded, giving the ladder to Caldwell, who unfolded a large plastic bag he had taken from his backpack and placed the ladder inside it. "A pretty good silversmith, but he was way over his head with this."

The man moved closer to John Sunspeaker. "Your family could have gotten a lot of money for this piece. You could have taken care of *your people* without even building a casino," he said, mocking him.

"Besides," Wellington added as he watched Caldwell seal the bag over the ladder, "the Natchez tribe isn't even a tribe anymore. What does it matter now if it's returned or not?"

"It belongs at the burial site," the nephew insisted.

"See, that's the trouble I have understanding you

people right there," Wellington commented. "That's exactly the problem with this entire story! Why would you want to recover this exquisite piece of art only to bury it in the ground?"

"Because it is where it belongs," John Sunspeaker replied.

"Well, now it belongs with me, and if makes you feel any better, I can promise you I will treat it with the utmost respect."

Wellington nodded at Caldwell and then started walking toward the house.

Caldwell motioned to the other two men to bring the Sunspeakers closer to the trio by the riverbank.

The two men pushed the family members down toward Rose. As they obeyed their orders and moved closer, she recognized them as the two men she had seen in the diner when she had stopped with Sheriff Montgomery on their way home from Checotah.

John and Daniel moved as they were directed. The older man had a sound look of defeat about him.

"Now, what do we do with so many of you?" Wellington had stopped and turned around to face them.

No one answered.

"Why don't you let the dead man's family go?" the sheriff finally said, trying to negotiate. He remained with his hands above his head. "And the woman," he added, referring to Rose. "Let them go and we can talk."

Wellington's right-hand man, Caldwell, smiled. "I don't think so, Sheriff."

He moved over to Rose and grinned in her face. "Ms. Rose Franklin, you know, we were so close yesterday to taking care of all of this, but now it looks like you've involved a lot of other people."

Wellington laughed.

Caldwell backed away and glanced around at his cohorts.

"Tie them up, too. We'll take them to the car."

The men forced John and Daniel to their knees. One of the pair stayed focused on them while the other pulled duct tape out of his pocket and began tying up the sheriff's hands first and then moved over to Rose. He shoved them both down next to the other hostages and then pulled Agent Lujan out of his seat. Clearly, the quick movement caused the injured man more pain, as he buckled to his knees, wrapping his arms around his waist.

Rose watched Caldwell's assistant pull him up and then tape his hands together behind his back. Lujan struggled to lift himself, and then the man kicked him over to where the others knelt.

Rose winced to see him in such agony and turned away so as not to face him directly. She could not imagine getting out of this situation with the same ease and good fortune she'd had when she was in the camper. She noticed the ax handle but knew that was no match for the three guns the other men had. She watched as the sheriff kept trying to negotiate.

"There's no need to keep all of us," he pleaded. "Just let them go."

"Shut up!" Wellington yelled, and everyone at the riverbank went silent.

That was when Rose heard the faint sound of a motorcycle. She struggled to listen and then she was certain. She heard more than just one, and the bikes were headed in their direction.

TWENTY-SEVEN

At first, it seemed to Rose that no one else noticed the approaching roar of the engines, but soon, it was evident that Wellington recognized help was on the way for his hostages.

He yelled for his associates to hurry the others up from the bank and through the woods, toward the house. Rose fell as she was being shoved along, but she was quickly pulled up and once again pushed forward. Even with the quickened pace, however, Wellington and the gunmen were not fast enough.

By the time they got to Sheriff Montgomery's house, the place was surrounded with what appeared to be a squad of Hell's Angels. Rose immediately recognized them as the gang that Lucas liked to ride with, the Welcome Wagon group.

There must have been twenty or more large men with lots of tattoos and plenty of attitude pulling up on motorcycles and moving in all directions. Only one deputy's car followed in behind them, but the siren blared as if a fleet of patrolmen were coming in.

"Get down," the sheriff yelled to Rose and the other hostages when he realized that there could be gunfire exchanged. The sheriff and the other four immediately dropped to the ground.

Wellington made a run for the SUV parked beside the camper, but Lucas jumped off his bike and tackled him before he made it to the door. When Caldwell and the other two men realized they were completely at a disadvantage, they dropped their weapons and raised their hands. The motorcycle riders circled them as the two deputies quickly moved in.

Sheriff Montgomery hurried over to one of the men on the motorcycles and gestured behind him at his taped wrists. The man immediately pulled out a knife and cut him loose. The sheriff then ran over, picked up Caldwell's firearm, and headed to where Lucas had his knee on Robert Wellington's neck and seemed to be bowed in prayer.

Rose wasn't sure whether it was a prayer of thanksgiving he was offering or one of forgiveness. Although it was obvious that he was doing the right thing in his rescue, Rose knew Lucas was not a violent man.

The sheriff handcuffed Wellington while the deputies took care of the other three.

"These men are under arrest for murder, kidnapping, burglary, possession of stolen goods, and"—he paused as they walked toward the car—"a slew of other crimes that I haven't even thought of yet."

He shoved them in the car and walked over to the other hostages. He borrowed the knife and began snapping off the tape from Rose, Agent Lujan, and finally the Sunspeaker men.

"You need me to call you an ambulance?" he asked Philip Lujan.

The agent shook his head and twisted a bit from side to side. "No, I think I'm feeling better now." He turned to Rose. "You got a mean swing, though," he said.

She rubbed her wrists. "Sorry about that."

"It's all right," he replied.

The Sunspeakers joined them as they gathered near the car where Lucas and the sheriff were already standing.

"How did you find out about all of this?" she asked Lucas. She reached up and hugged her friend, shaking her head in disbelief.

"Willie," Lucas said.

Rose was puzzled.

"Willie saw the SUV in the campground this afternoon. It pulled in next to the big rig from California," he explained.

"Wellington," Rose added.

The others leaned in to hear.

Lucas nodded. "He remembered that it was the second car that had entered Shady Grove the night the man from New Mexico was murdered." He turned to John and Daniel Sunspeaker, both of whom were listening. "I'm sorry," he said to the two men, appearing as if he knew they were family.

They nodded at Lucas.

"Anyway," he said, getting back to the story, "Willie came over to the office, where Rhonda and I were, and told us. So when those fellows left, I followed the vehicle over to the motel and could tell right away there was more trouble about to break."

Rose was enjoying hearing his account of things.

"I called some friends, ran into Deputy Dog over there on Second Street, where the gang was gathering, and he said you had come by the office and were heading out here." He pointed with his chin over to some of the motorcycle riders. "Rhonda's there."

Rose searched among the other riders and found her friend as she removed her helmet. Her red hair fell out on her shoulders. They smiled at each other.

"I told her to stay at Shady Grove, but she said if you were here, she was coming." Lucas winked at his wife, who waved in response. "She thinks of you like a sister."

Rose nodded. She felt exactly the same way.

"So that's what happened."

Rose reached up, hugging Lucas again. "Where would I be without you?" she said.

John Sunspeaker searched around the grounds, trying to locate the ladder. When he did, he went over, picked it up, took it out of the plastic bag, and handed it to Agent Lujan. "My uncle understood that you would know what to do with this," he said.

Agent Lujan nodded. He took the ladder from the dead man's nephew. "He called me a long time ago to say he had been troubled by a dream, a dream of restless spirits."

Hearing that, Rose remembered the dream she'd had when she was in the stolen camper. She realized it was the same one the dead man had dreamed. She walked closer to hear the conversation.

The agent continued. "He told me about an old ladder that his family had passed down from generation to generation but that had been lost or stolen many years ago."

John Sunspeaker nodded, already knowing the story. "He knew it had come from an ancestor who had escaped the terrible slaughter in Louisiana, the extinction of the Natchez people."

Rose had read this story while she had been researching at the library. She knew that there had been almost five thousand people in that tribe, that their ruler was the Great Sun, and that he lived in a huge dwelling on a high, flat-topped mound. She remembered reading the account from 1729. The French attacked the tribe, trying to gain control of the leader's home. The entire tribe had been destroyed. She knew that most had been killed or taken as slaves but that a few had survived and fled the region.

Based upon the comments the nephew had made, she assumed that Mr. Sunspeaker's ancestor had been one of those who became a refugee in the Southwest, that he must have become a part of the Zuni tribe, another pueblo people who believed their high priest and political chief was a descendant of the Great Sun.

She listened to the two men as they continued talking.

"Our ancestor brought with him pieces of strong wood and stones from his leader's fallen home. He was to build the ladder for the lost spirits of his people. The story goes that the ladder had to be built and then returned to Natchez and that without it the spirits of the people could not find their way home." John Sunspeaker looked over at the ladder he had handed to Philip Lujan.

"My mother's brother was troubled for a very long time. He served in the war and came back to the pueblo as a man broken, lost. He was taken to prison, always in fights, always drunk. And then he received the vision to find and return the ladder to Natchez.

"From that time on, he searched for it. He was a new man, a man with purpose. Once he found the ladder stored away in some museum, he replaced all of the missing stones that had been stolen, and he knew he would see it returned to its rightful place. It was all he lived for."

Agent Lujan held the ladder reverently.

John Sunspeaker lowered his head and a breeze poured through the trees. It was a passing wind that shifted through budding limbs and stirred the piles of cold, wet leaves. And just as swiftly as it came, it went. It seemed to Rose that it signaled the easy passage of a captured soul, suddenly released.

"There is this, as well," the sheriff said, breaking the silence. He walked over to the dead man's nephew and handed him the bracelet Rose had found.

The man smiled and took the piece of jewelry, then placed it in his son's hands. They nodded at each other and spoke softly in the Zuni language. The father slid his arm across the younger man's neck; then a silence fell between them.

John Sunspeaker then turned to the group gathered around him. "We thank you for taking care to find our uncle's murderers, for securing the ladder, and for helping us find peace for our journey home."

Rose considered the long trip they still had ahead of them as they returned to New Mexico. She considered inviting them for dinner, since the hour was late, but then she remembered that she didn't really have anything to offer them. Her cupboard was bare, she recalled.

And then just as she had that thought, Thomas, Ms. Lou Ellen, and Mary pulled up in Ms. Lou Ellen's car. Thomas jumped out and ran over to Rose.

"Are you all right?" he asked, reaching for her.

She felt his arms around her once again. "I am now," she said.

"Rose, dear," Ms. Lou Ellen was calling out as she emerged from the car. "If you don't refrain from this dangerous behavior, I swear I am going to be as big as the side of a house. I can't keep expecting to hear bad news and finding it necessary to eat so much." She moved in Rose's direction. "Because if you continue being involved in this kind of harm, we will one day finally be celebrating your funeral." She reached over and pinched her friend roughly on the arm.

Rose pulled her arm away and rubbed it. She grimaced. "Yes, ma'am," she replied.

Lucas and Thomas laughed.

Rose remembered that she wanted to offer dinner to the men visiting West Memphis. She had an idea.

"How about let's put an end to all of this death talk and eat all that funeral food tonight?" she said. "Let's just get rid of it and forget completely about any more anticipatory grief."

"You got folks in mind to share all that with?" Lucas asked, remembering how much food there still was at his mother-in-law's house.

"Absolutely," Rose replied, turning in the direction of the three men from out of state.

"Well, where are my manners?" said Ms. Lou Ellen, holding out her hand to the men standing by Rose.

Suddenly, Mary opened the rear door of the car and the three-legged dog jumped from the backseat and ran over to Daniel Sunspeaker.

The young man reached down and picked up his great-uncle's pet. "Look, Dad," he said to his father, "it's Lucky."

Ms. Lou Ellen and Rose watched as both men petted the one they had come to know as Lester Earl.

Mary walked over to the group. "This your dog?" she asked Daniel.

The young man nodded. "He was a family pet," he said, "Lucky."

"You take him with you?" Mary asked, surprising everyone with her question. The concern in her voice could not be masked.

The three-legged mutt jumped from the boy's arms and limped over to the women. Without a word, it was Mary who immediately scooped him up and gave him a big kiss. Ms. Lou Ellen and Rose watched in amazement.

"I guess Lucky is still lucky," the young man's father responded. "He should stay here, since I expect he will be happier," he added. "He has always fancied the arms of women."

Mary smiled at the answer, while Ms. Lou Ellen, simply and elegantly, threw back her head and laughed out loud.

TWENTY-EIGHT

Rose's decision to return to Rocky Mount had nothing to do with a feeling of obligation or duty and everything to do with the solving of a murder. She was guided by the dream from an old man's ladder.

She thought about it all night after her friends had gathered to eat every morsel cooked by Ms. Lou Ellen in loving preparation for Rose's funeral. She had stayed later than she had planned and then walked home, stuffed and satisfied and at peace with where she was and how things had turned out.

The Sunspeaker men, the nephew and great-nephew of the man who bore a burdensome dream, joined them for food and drink, speaking only sparingly as the group from Shady Grove prodded them with questions and too many stories of their own.

Rose had asked about the bracelet, about a funeral for the elder, and about their lives in the pueblo. The bracelet was to go to the great-nephew, a link in the chain of the male relatives. It told, as she had suspected, the story of the Natchez people, the story of Jacob's ladder. The elder Sunspeaker had made the piece of jewelry after he had received the first dream, when he first began to understand his quest.

The funeral was not discussed, as the subject of death was not for idle conversation among the family members of the deceased. As for their lives in New Mexico, John Sunspeaker simply acknowledged the vast openness of the desert landscape, saying that it was the only home he and his family knew. He extended an open invitation for Rose and the others to visit his pueblo at any time.

Philip Lujan had been the one to show the two men the exact location where their loved one had died. The three of them stayed by the river for more than an hour, and they returned only briefly for the meal and some conversation before leaving for their respective homes.

When it came time for Rose to depart from the gathering of friends, it was obvious to everyone that she had been affected in some unexplained way by the three men's silent strength and by their resolve to honor their familial ties. Although no one but Thomas understood the decision she was making, once the night was over, everyone saw that she had made up her mind about something.

She walked hand in hand with Thomas, noticing the trail to her right, the one that led up to the site where Mr. Jacob Sunspeaker had parked, the place where he had died. She stood looking for a moment, curious about what the younger men had done there, almost walking down to see, and then finally understanding the sacredness of their good-byes. She knew not to trespass upon it.

Instead, she turned to walk forward on her own journey. Without bearing right and moving toward her travel trailer, her home, she moved straight down to the banks of the muddy Mississippi, lifted her face in the air, breathing in the late-night river smells, and sat down.

Thomas joined her, his arm securely around her, and at the moment he pulled her closer to him, she announced what she was going to do. She faced the city opposite them, the land over east, as if it she were announcing it to the people there, as well.

Thomas said nothing when she explained. He only nodded his head in understanding. He offered to take her, said he'd ride next to her and stay with her for as long as she planned to be there.

She smiled at the offer, sat with the tenderness of it,

let the proposal of such a thing flow across her mind. Then she turned to him with complete clarity.

"No," she said. "This is mine to do alone."

He did not reply. He understood that part of her decision, as well. Later, as they stood at her camper and said good night, they held each other a little longer than usual, knowing it would be more than a few days before they would see each other again.

She drove out of Shady Grove early the next morning. Old Man Willie waved at her from his front porch. He was the only one she saw as she left. The lights were still out at the cabin and the office, and she hesitated at first to leave without saying goodbye. She knew, however, that she would be coming back, so she just moved out slowly so as not to wake her friends.

Thomas would tell the others soon enough, she knew. And they would be waiting when she was ready to come home.

She took the turn out of the campground, watching from the rearview mirror, glad she had such a place to return to. She put on her seat belt just as she merged on the interstate and settled in for the long drive she had in front of her.

She sped through Memphis without radio or taped music, noticing that the town was only just starting to show signs of a morning commute. She drove on to Jackson and Nashville, enjoying the silence and the grand arrival of dawn, before she finally decided to stop and take a break.

She pulled off the interstate just as the sun was high and full, welcoming the beginning of a new day. She gassed up, got a sweet roll and a cup of coffee, and stood outside her car, watching the traffic pick up along I-40, heading both east and west.

It was, she realized, a beautiful spring morning, so full of possibility. She glanced in her backseat, remembering that she had packed a few things, not sure how long she would stay, not sure of what she would take as a sign that she could leave, that she had completed her task. She understood, however, as she contemplated the trip, that this was a journey not about days or hours or a need to be finished; it was a journey as important as one from world to world, life to death.

She stood in the early-morning sunshine, remembering the conversation she'd had with Thomas the night before, the way he'd slid his finger along the sides of her face, the way they'd leaned into each other, the way he'd promised to be in North Carolina in less than a day if she called him, if she needed him, if she just wanted to see him.

She smiled, the warmth of the season pressing down upon her, because she was relieved of the burden she had carried so long. She felt different than she ever had; she felt free.

Somehow in the hearing of the dead man's story, in watching the exchange of the ladder from John Sunspeaker to Philip Lujan, in realizing the price that the old man, Jacob, had paid to give passage to long-abandoned and lost souls, she felt chosen, called like he, to give a restless spirit a place to begin and end.

Jacob's ladder, Rose thought, recalling the story from the Old Testament, is just what Thomas said it is. It is the mercy that shows up like a dream in the fretful night while lost in the wilderness, a dream that comforts, a dream that promises that even though you are running for your life, unsettled, desperate, unforgiven, one day you will find true rest, one day you will find your way home.

Rose understood that her father would more than likely not even recognize her, might not even know that it was he who had called her back to North Carolina to grant the forgiveness that would be his ladder, his vehicle to start him on his way home. She knew that he would probably deny that it was his soul that spoke to her in dreams.

Rose walked away from where she had been standing, threw her trash in the garbage can at the side of the station, and returned to the driver's seat of her car.

"It doesn't matter," Rose said to herself as she buckled the seat belt and pulled into the Tennessee traffic. "I'm not just going for him."

She merged into the morning commute without being impatient about the traffic or about what she might not find when she stood at her father's bedside. She had learned a great lesson from Jacob and from his commitment to return the ladder to the Natchez tribe.

On the morning of her return trip to North Carolina, Rose recalled the quest of the old man from New Mexico and the way he had devoted himself completely to returning the ladder to the lost souls. She also remembered how she felt when his nephew handed the ladder to Agent Lujan.

Rose thought of that moment when they stood in the sudden breeze as she drove along in the slow progress of traffic, how it seemed so clearly to be the perfect and final release of a restless soul.

Rose understood that, just as it had been for Jacob Sunspeaker, the man who discovered purpose in a dream and wholeness in the fulfillment of a three-hundred-year-old promise, as we allow ourselves to become the vehicle of grace for another, we are merely securing the rungs of the ladder that guarantees our own sweet passage home.

She smiled and moved ahead.

Center Point Publishing
600 Brooks Road • PO Box 1
Thorndike ME 04986-0001 USA

(207) 568-3717

US & Canada:
1 800 929-9108
www.centerpointlargeprint.com